DIE HARD
WITH A VENGEANCE

TWENTIETH CENTURY FOX PRESENTS

IN ASSOCIATION WITH CINERGI AN ANDREW G. VAJNA PRODUCTION A JOHN McTIERNAN FILM BRUCE WILLIS JEREMY IRONS SAMUEL

VENGEANCE GRAHAM GREENE DP CARMINE ZOZZORA MENZIES AND JOHN McTIERNAN

COLLEEN CAMP LARRY BREGMAN SAM PHILLIPS MUSIC MICHAEL KAMEN EDITED BY JOHN WRIGHT A.C.E. MICHAEL R. MILLER A.C.E. DESIGNER JA

DAVID WILLIS EXECUTIVE PRODUCERS ANDREW G. VAJNA, BUZZ FEITSHANS, ROBERT LAWRENCE WRITTEN BY JONATHAN HENSLEIGH P

CINERGI.

D1462654

DIE HARD
WITH A VENGEANCE

A novel by D. CHIEL
Based on a screenplay written by JONATHAN HENSLEIGH

SMP

ST. MARTIN'S PAPERBACKS

DIE HARD WITH A VENGEANCE

Copyright © 1995 by Twentieth Century Fox Film Corporation.

Cover photograph copyright © 1995 by Twentieth Century Fox Film Corporation.

ISBN: 0-312-95676-2

Printed in the United States of America

St. Martin's Paperbacks edition / May 1995

10 9 8 7 6 5 4 3 2

For Marci Knight, and Sarah, Sean, and Ira Udow

Chapter 1

At dawn, the sun was a brilliant orange ball of fire rising in the pale blue sky above New York City. It hovered for a few brief moments at the point where the horizon merged with the East River, casting a ghostly silverish tint across the water that separated Manhattan from its sister boroughs, Queens and Brooklyn. The temperature had stayed close to the eighty-degree mark throughout the night, with only a faint breeze that smelled of fish and the ocean to cool the air. A trio of sea gulls dove beneath the gently ruffled waves, then quickly resurfaced, screeching as they wheeled toward the sun, now visible between the two arching steel spans of the Brooklyn Bridge.

The city was slowly coming awake. From Inwood and Washington Heights at the island's northernmost reaches all the way south to Wall

Street's narrow canyons, people were stretching and yawning and shaking off sleep. Uptown, the runners trying to beat the heat dripped sweat as they pounded the track that circled the Central Park Reservoir. On the Upper West Side, along the length of Broadway, the Korean greengrocers rearranged their sidewalk displays of fresh fruits and flowers. Delivery trucks dropped off bales of *The New York Times* at the sidewalk kiosks so news-hungry New Yorkers could get their daily fix of politics, culture, sports, and disaster.

In midtown, commuters began trickling out of the subway stations, stopping just long enough to buy a cup of coffee and a doughnut from one of the cart vendors on Lexington or Third Avenues to the east, Sixth or Seventh to the west. Bearded Hasidic merchants, dressed in their traditional garb of wide-brimmed hats and long black coats, greeted one another in Yiddish as they hurried toward their shops in the diamond district along West Forty-seventh Street. Further downtown, lawyers and security traders were clad in their own particular corporate uniform of pinstripes, ties, and suspenders as they headed for the air-conditioned comfort zones of their high-rise office buildings near the courts and stock exchanges.

Summer in New York. The humidity gets trapped between the office buildings. The air grows thick and gritty with dirt, sticking to the palms and cheeks and forehead like an extra layer of skin. The streets and sidewalks feel like ovens. The homicide rate soars. The heat makes the sane crazy, and pushes the crazies so far over the edge they might never regain their balance.

It was too early for all but the most dedicated tourists to be out, though soon enough the hordes would emerge from hotels all over the city, clutching their cameras and guidebooks. Traffic on Fifth Avenue, New York's great north-south thoroughfare, was just starting to move toward gridlock. Shoppers were heading for Bloomie's, Macy's, Saks Fifth Avenue, and the rest of New York's department stores.

Bonwit Teller, one of the most elegant of the stores, drew visitors from all over the world, some of whom came to shop, others simply to sightsee. The handsome brick building had for decades dominated the corner of Fifty-seventh and Fifth, one of New York's great shopping crossroads. The store hadn't yet opened for the day's business when it was suddenly rocked by an explosion that was terrifying in its violence and intensity.

The building shuddered and heaved, then collapsed inward as though a tornado had suddenly hit in that one, isolated spot. The ground shook from the force of the blast, buckling the adjoining sidewalks. Glass and brick flew in every direction. A cloud of dust and smoke rose high in the air and billowed out into the streets.

The day shift had just begun at the New York Police Department Headquarters when news of the explosion came crackling over the switchboard. From the force of the blast and extent of damage, the first cops to arrive on the scene were betting that it was a bomb. "Blown to smithereens," was how one of them described the building when he'd called in his report. Had the explosion occurred half an hour later, the sidewalk would have been thick with pedestrians rushing to work. Hundreds could have been injured or killed.

A Con Edison team was already racing to the scene, just in case a gas leak had caused the devastation. It would take the combined efforts of all the investigators to determine the precise cause, but for now the cops were sticking with the bomb theory.

In the detectives' bullpen, Chief of Detectives Walter Cobb was barking commands. His people checked their guns, grabbed jackets and notepads, and gulped down one more sip of coffee before they headed uptown.

No one had claimed credit yet for the bombing, which meant that the field was wide open. The explosion at the World Trade Center was on everyone's mind. But terrorists weren't the only ones who liked to play with dynamite. On any given day, all kinds of lunatics were on the loose in New York; anyone with a grudge and enough brains to wire together a couple of sticks and an alarm clock could be responsible for the damage at Bonwit's.

Ricky Walsh, the friendly baby-faced newcomer to the squad, asked the question everyone else had been wondering. "Bonwit's? What's anybody got against Bonwit's?"

"Ever see a woman miss a shoe sale?" cracked Joe Lambert, who chose to mask his sharp intelligence with an endless stream of bad jokes.

Connie Kowalski, a self-described "pushy little broad from Brooklyn," scowled in response. Before she had a chance to respond to her colleague, Chief Cobb's secretary, Jane, yelled above the clatter, "Walter! Phone!"

Cobb ignored her and continued issuing orders. "Alan," he said. "You start the notifications—bomb squad, special services, state police, and FBI. Jackson and Parma—St. John's Emergency Room in case they get any walk-ins. Cramer, get with the city engineer's office. Find out if we've got collateral damage, if we have to evacuate surrounding buildings, and so on. Donovan, you liaise with the mayor's office. Connie, get started on the witness sheet. Ricky and Joe, make sure the uniforms have sealed it at three blocks. And keep the TV crews the hell out!"

He grimaced, picturing the panic that would ensue if the image of Bonwit's, now reduced to a huge pile of rubble and dust, were to be broadcast across the tristate area on the morning news. He was fighting a losing battle; an explosion in midtown was a major story, important enough to merit a break in regular programming for the inevitable high-tech graphics, followed by live on-the-spot coverage. His only hope was to delay the inevitable, until he had some information to prevent anyone from panicking.

Glancing up, he noticed his secretary waving at him from across the room. "Not now!" He shook his head at her and looked around to see who was still available. "Benson," he said, "you take the traffic department. If we can't get Sixth Avenue opened by three, we're gonna have the rush hour from hell."

Jane hurried over to him. "Walter!" she said, more urgently this time. "He says he set the bomb at Bonwit Teller."

She pointed to the telephone, but with all the confusion in the room, it took a couple of seconds for the words to register. He bolted for the relative quiet of his office and snatched the phone from its cradle. "Major Case Unit. Cobb," he said into the receiver.

The voice at the other end was as cold and dry as a crisp white wine. Cobb couldn't put a face to the voice, and the message was stranger still.

"Simple Simon met a pieman, / Going to the fair," the voice recited in a European accent.

Cobb strained to place the exact country of origin as the man went on, "Said Simple Simon to the pieman, / 'Give me your pies—or I'll cave your goddamn head in.'"

There was a brief pause, as if the caller were waiting for Cobb to react to the punch line.

Cobb had thought he'd heard it all, but sicko nursery rhymes were a new one on him. He held his breath, waiting for the caller to get to the point. Hoping that he wouldn't hang up until he let slip whatever piece of information had impelled him to call in the first place. Some perps couldn't wait to confess. Others liked to tease and tantalize. Still others were simply nut bars who got their rocks off by taking credit for other people's crimes. Often, Cobb could guess from the sound of the voice which category a caller fit into. This time, the accent threw him off.

"Is there a detective named McClane there?"

The question was just about the last one Cobb had expected to hear. McClane? What the hell did this guy want with Johnny? Cobb groaned silently. If he and McClane were friends, they were really in trouble.

"He's on suspension," he said flatly.

"No, Walter." The European-accented voice just as flatly contradicted him. "Not today."

A very bad situation was quickly taking a sharp

turn for the worse. "Who is this?" Cobb demanded.

"Call me Simon," the voice replied. Then he said, "Bonwit Teller was just for show."

Possibly a terrorist. Definitely a lunatic. Cobb felt a sharp stabbing sensation in his belly, the start of what promised to develop into a very nasty attack of ulcers. "What do you want?" he asked, digging in his pocket for his antacid tablets.

"To play a game."

As a kid, Cobb had never been big on games. He liked them even less as an adult, especially when they involved the destruction of valuable real estate and potentially lethal explosive devices. "What kind of game?" he said warily.

"Simon Says." The man who had identified himself as Simon spoke in a low, sinister tone that demanded to be taken seriously. Cobb searched his memory, trying to recall anything that could link the accent or the voice with previous explosions. When he came up blank, he pictured McClane and repeated the exercise. The pain in his gut worsened, as so often happened when he thought about John McClane.

"In the next few hours," the caller said, "Simon's going to tell Detective McClane what to do and Detective McClane is going to do it. Noncompliance will result in a penalty."

"What penalty?"

"Ten pounds of explosives in a very public place."

Cobb swallowed hard. After all these years on the force, he'd learned to distinguish the idle wacko threats from the real thing. Simon might be crazy, but he was on the level crazy. Cobb had absolutely no doubt that he meant business. He was ready to bet his detective's gold shield on that.

He covered the phone with his hand and yelled into the other room. "Lambert! Kowalski! You know where McClane is?"

The two detectives glanced at each other as they stepped into his office.

Lambert shrugged. "He ain't in church," he said, smirking.

Cobb generally got a kick out of Lambert's sarcastic humor. Life could look pretty grim from behind the chief of detectives' desk, and Joe had a way of lightening up the atmosphere. Right now, though, he wasn't in the mood for any wisecracks. Mr. Simon Pieman, whoever the hell he was, didn't sound like the patient type, and ten pounds of explosives could do more damage than Cobb cared to contemplate.

"Well, find what rock he's under and turn him over," he barked at the two detectives. "And take Walsh with you."

"Wait!" Kowalski protested. "What about Bonwit's?"

He glared at her. She was a good detective, smart and gutsy as any of the men on the squad, but her big mouth too often got in her way. "Don't argue, Connie! Go!" he barked at her and Lambert. He took a deep breath to calm himself and removed his hand from the receiver. "What is it you want McClane to do?" he asked the caller.

"Simon says Detective McClane is to go to the corner of 138th Street and Amsterdam. That's in Harlem, if I'm not mistaken."

Cobb sighed and wondered why, of all the 31,000 cops in the city, this Simon character had to choose John McClane to do his bidding. McClane . . . who followed orders only when it suited him to do so, reveled in flaunting authority, attracted trouble like steel filings to a magnet. And why now, when McClane was as close as he'd ever been to getting himself kicked off the force?

Johnny was a hard case, no question about it. He was a classic, a cop from the old school of "shoot first, ask questions later." He was also probably the most fearless man Cobb had ever met, which didn't always work in his favor. Everyone, cops most especially, needed to know the sour, slightly metallic taste of fear to protect them from situations where a moment of caution meant all the difference between a pension after twenty years and a posthumous award for bravery.

McClane, however, seemed to thrive on the dizzying thrill that came from taking risks. He was like a drug addict, craving danger to make him feel alive. And like a drug addict, when he came down from the high, he was out of control, his life was a mess.

He'd started to fall apart when his wife had accepted a new job that meant moving herself and the kids out to Los Angeles. He'd gone to see her, the first Christmas they'd been living apart, and almost got himself killed when a gang of terrorists had taken over the high-rise office building where she worked. He'd saved a lot of lives that day and wound up a hero. He'd been written up in *People* and interviewed on *Nightline*. Cobb smiled, recalling the spectacle of poor Ted Koppel trying to get a straight answer out of McClane.

He wondered whether Lambert would remember to pick up a container of coffee for McClane. Chances were better than good that John was either recovering from last night's hangover or getting an early start on a new one. He'd been warned for the third and final time that if he didn't get help staying off the booze, he'd have to permanently turn in his badge and gun.

A lush, a madman, and ten pounds of explosives. When was he going to take his wife's ad-

vice and put in for retirement? His gut was on
fire. He opened his drawer, found his roll of ant-
acids, and popped three in his mouth. This was
turning out to be one hell of a crappy day.

Lambert knocked on McClane's door, four sharp
raps that were followed by silence. He tried
again, more loudly. Again, nothing. Kowalski
nudged him out of the way and pounded on the
door with her fist. Still, no response, though only
a dead man could ignore the racket they were
making. Walsh stepped up to take a turn, but Kowalski shook her head. If McClane was home, he
obviously wasn't in the mood for company. They
were wasting their time, waiting for him to invite
them inside.

   She stepped backwards a couple of paces,
aimed herself at the door, and waited for Lambert
and Walsh to line up alongside her. On the count
of three, they hurled themselves forward, grunting as their shoulders made contact with the thick
wooden surface. The door crashed inward, splin-
tering halfway off the frame, so that they stumbled and almost fell into McClane's apartment.

   Kowalski had been there once before, and the
place hadn't exactly looked like the Plaza Hotel,
but she still wasn't prepared for the chaos that
greeted them. McClane had moved into the apartment after Holly had left, and he'd never gotten
around to buying more than the most basic pieces

of furniture. The decor was early bachelor: a
ratty-looking couch with cigarette burns; a rick-
ety coffee table that was covered with overflow-
ing ashtrays, crumpled beer cans, and a couple
of half-empty pizza boxes. Bedsheets doubled as
curtains for the windows, and the floor was lit-
tered with socks, underwear, and other items of
clothing.

A shirt was draped over the only lamp in the
room, a pair of pants across the top of the televi-
sion set that was tuned to live coverage of the
bombing. The flickering image on the screen pro-
vided the only light in the otherwise darkened
room, which faced another apartment across a
narrow courtyard.

Kowalski stared at the stylishly dressed news
reporter pointing grimly at the giant pile of rubble that once had been Bonwit's. The chief must
be pissed. He'd said no TV crews, and now all of
New York was being offered front-row seats at
the scene. Somebody wasn't doing his job, and
there'd be hell to pay back at the office, which
made the situation here with McClane all the
more urgent.

"You ever smell anything like this?" asked
Walsh, holding his nose.

Lambert shook his head. "Once. At the
morgue."

He was exaggerating, but just slightly. Despite
the heat, the window had been opened only a

couple of inches. The place reeked of stale smoke, spilled booze, and garbage that should have been thrown away a week ago. Kowalski bent to pick up a container of milk that lay on its side, thought better of it as she got a whiff of its soured contents, and looked up to find McClane yawning at them from the doorway of his bedroom.

"Hey, fellas," he said, lighting a cigarette. He seemed not the least bit surprised by their presence, as if people breaking into his apartment first thing in the morning was a part of his regular routine.

He was wearing shorts and a tank top skimpy enough to reveal that despite a steady diet of booze, cigarettes, and junk food, he'd somehow managed to stay in decent shape. But his short hair, tousled from sleep, was beginning to go gray at the temples, and his eyes were badly bloodshot.

Kowalski stared at him in dismay. "Jesus, John," she said.

How could such a good cop let himself get into such an awful mess?

McClane was so hung over that Walsh and Lambert had to prop him up in the shower, dress him, and half-carry him out to the car. They threw him into the back seat and assigned Walsh, because he was the most junior member of the team, the job of keeping him propped up and more or less awake until they got downtown.

Cobb had told them to radio ahead, and he had the van waiting and ready to go as soon as they arrived. Whatever Simon's game might be, Cobb wanted to get on with playing it. He didn't like the idea of using McClane as a decoy. But he couldn't sit back and wait for ten pounds of explosives to detonate, and Simon hadn't yet given him anything else to work with.

He liked the idea even less as the van sped uptown to Harlem. McClane was . . . how old now? . . . had to be close to forty, which meant Cobb had known him for almost twenty years. He was still a handsome son-of-a-bitch, even with the lines in his face that testified to his hard living. But he looked tired, weighed down with the kind of soul-weariness that settles deep into the bones and needs more than a good night's sleep to cure.

He sat with his eyes closed, his head leaning against the side. Every time the van hit a bump in the street, McClane's head bounced backwards against the wall. He didn't seem to feel the pain. The man didn't even flinch.

"Jesus, John. You look like shit," he said succinctly.

McClane's eyes flickered open, exposing redrimmed lids. "What do you want me to do, Walter? Comb my hair?"

He motioned to Kowalski, who handed him a

large cup of coffee, black. Lambert passed her a
bottle of aspirin, and she doled out four to Mc-
Clane.

"More," he said.

Kowalski put two more into the palm of his
outstretched hand. When he nodded at her to
keep going, she reluctantly added another two.

Cobb's stomach ached just from watching Mc-
Clane swallow the eight aspirins with coffee. It
was a medical miracle that John didn't have a
bleeding ulcer by now. The insides of his belly
had to be lined with steel.

Cobb turned back to Walsh. "Keep going with
the roster," he said.

"Three killings in Red Hook the last two
nights."

Whatever Simple Simon had up his sleeve, it
was still business as usual in the rest of the city.
The neighborhood of Red Hook, in the northwest
corner of Brooklyn, had become a real trouble
spot in the last few years. A beloved elementary
school principle had been shot to death when
he'd accidentally stepped into the crossfire of two
drug dealers. The local residents were demanding
increased police presence, an end to the random
violence. Cobb suspected that the most recent
murders were drug-related, but were the three
connected?

"Put Miner on it. And Genetti. The mayor's

office will be calling before the day's out," he said.

The mayor had run on a law-and-order agenda, and he'd brought in a tough, street-smart police commissioner who demanded results. The two men shared a passion for statistics that proved they were winning the fight against crime. A hat trick of killings in forty-eight hours was bad PR for the department and the city.

"Next," said Walsh, making notes on his printout. "Fourteen dump trucks stolen from a yard on Staten Island." He looked up from the sheet. "*Fourteen?* Somebody going into the construction business?"

"John's landlady was gonna clean his apartment," Lambert said, not skipping a beat.

Kowalski and Walsh broke up laughing, and Cobb managed a smile.

"Insurance fraud," said McClane, massaging his temples.

They stared at him. Even in this state, he was still a step ahead of the rest of them.

He opened his eyes and lit a cigarette. "By now the trucks are in California, and the contractor's collecting insurance, which he'll split with the thieves. They've run it in Jersey for years."

Cobb sighed. John McClane was the best cop he'd ever worked with. A mind like a computer, a memory like an elephant's, a steady hand with a gun. A loner and a hot dog who always had to have it his way. Now, a drunk, and soon, an ex-cop.

"See if Kelly can do anything with it," Cobb told Walsh.

Walsh jotted Kelly's name next to the line reporting the dump truck thefts and stuck the print-out in his pocket. A thick silence fell in the van as the detectives focused their attention on Mc-Clane and his rendezvous with the mysterious caller.

McClane sensed their tension. "Is it hot in here or am I just scared to death?" he asked, trying to lighten up the atmosphere.

Kowalski, the first one to realize he was kidding, laughed nervously. Walsh and Lambert joined in. Cobb sighed again, regretting the waste of all that good training and instinct.

McClane smiled thinly. "Anyone know the lottery number last night?"

"Four-four-six-seven," they replied, a chorus of disappointed lottery players who lived from drawing to drawing, always hoping to hit the jackpot that would free them from their financial worries.

"Still playing your badge number, Ricky?" asked McClane.

Walsh nodded sheepishly. "Six-nine-one-one, every week."

" 'Six-nine-one-one, every week.' " McClane echoed Walsh. He chuckled, a low, dry sound at the back of his throat. "Christ! Half the cops in New York are betting their badge numbers."

"How are the kids, John?" Cobb changed the subject.

McClane scowled. "I *hear* they're doing okay," he said.

Cobb felt badly for him. It had to be tough for John to have his two kids a continent away. A cute little boy and girl, Cobb recalled, though they probably weren't so little anymore. Kids had a way of growing too quickly, especially if you didn't get to see them more than a couple of times a year.

The driver swung a sharp left turn. "Coming up on it, Captain," he said.

"You sure the gun's secure?" Cobb asked.

McClane slipped off his T-shirt and reached behind to touch the pistol that was taped to his back. "It's in the lower part of my back, doc," he said. "Some kind of growth." He winked at Kowalski as he pulled off his trousers. "You're the first woman since Holly who's seen me do this."

"I'm honored," she said drily.

"So was she . . . at first."

Cobb frowned. He hadn't planned to bring up the subject, not now, with tensions already high and so much at stake. But he didn't want McClane taking any dumb chances. Nor did he want him to use this assignment as a God-given excuse to self-destruct. It seemed like an opportune moment to remind him that he was still a police officer, with responsibilities both to the department and himself.

"John," he said sternly. "You don't get this business with Holly behind you, I won't be able to do diddly at the hearing."

McClane wasn't hearing any of it. "You're pulling back to 125th Street?" he said, as the driver braked to a stop.

"He said no cops in ten blocks," Cobb explained. He frowned again, wishing that John would give him the slightest sign that he wasn't about to embark on a kamikaze mission. That he understood the dangers he was about to face.

As if responding to Cobb's unspoken concerns, McClane suddenly said, "What the hell is this about, Walter? And why me?"

Cobb had been asking himself the very same questions ever since Simon had called. He'd hoped that McClane might have some answers—or at least the beginnings of a theory. He shook his head. "I have no idea. He just said you."

"Nice to be needed," said McClane, sounding as if he could have cared less that Simon might be setting him up to use as target practice.

His glib tone got the better of Cobb, who was fed up with making excuses for him to his superiors. "Frankly, John, you haven't been a lot of use to anyone since you and Holly—"

"Walter, enough, okay?" McClane cut him off. "Between you, her, and this clown Simon . . . you're screwing up a good hangover."

He jerked open the back door of the van and stepped into the street, dressed only in his socks, boxer shorts, and strudy black cop shoes.

Cobb peered uneasily to the left and right, searching for signs of Simon's presence in the vicinity. He wondered why Simon had picked Harlem, and why this particular street, one of the most rundown in the neighborhood. The block was lined with decrepit, sagging brownstones, alongside a bar, a shabby-looking laundromat, an appliance-repair shop, and a small grocery store. The corpse of what once had been a car was parked in front of the laundromat. Its hood was flung open to reveal its missing innards. The tires had been stripped, the windows smashed, and what was left of the body was covered in graffiti.

A window shade in an apartment across the street snapped open. Cobb jerked his head upward, searching for a pair of eyes, the glint of a gun, the face of his caller. A skinny black-and-white cat leaped onto the window sill, arched its back, and howled, then retreated into the shadows beyond the open window.

The street was empty, except for a pair of junkies nodding out in the doorway of the grocery store. Still scanning up and down the block, Cobb handed McClane a large white sandwich board, created precisely to Simon's specifications.

McClane pulled the board over his head and adjusted the straps that held the two pieces together, so that the weight was evenly distributed across his shoulders.

"It's a little short in the sleeves, but I like the lapels," he said, baring his teeth in what could pass for a smile. "Get me one in suede and I'll pick it up Thursday."

Cobb glanced around one last time, but saw nothing in the urban landscape worth noting. Wherever Simon had hidden himself, he was keeping a low profile.

"We'll be back to get you in fifteen minutes," he said, trying to sound more encouraging then he felt.

"Don't bother. I expect I'll be dead in five," McClane announced in his usual deadpan fashion.

His parting crack was exactly what Cobb didn't need to hear right now. He was a lot more worried about McClane than he cared to admit. The major part of his concern came from knowing that, on some level, John didn't give a damn whether he lived or died. That kind of attitude was what got other cops killed.

Almost every day, there was a story in the papers about yet another cop with a lousy home life who'd stuck a gun in his mouth and blown out his brains. But Cobb had been on the force long enough to know a cop could kill himself and make it look like he'd died a hero's death. Not that McClane looked like much of a hero, standing in the middle of the street, wearing only the sandwich board and his shorts.

Cobb shook his head and signaled the driver to move. Simon had said he would tell McClane what to do next, which seemed to indicate he was planning to keep him alive. All Cobb could do now was hope and pray that Simon would stick to the rules of his game.

Chapter 2

McClane watched the van make a U-turn, head south, and disappear from view. He stared down over the front of the sandwich board at his shoes and socks and realized he hadn't felt so humiliated since his old man had showed up drunk at his eighth birthday party. Watching his father stumble around their tiny backyard, he'd begun to realize that he could love and hate someone at the same time. It had been a hard lesson to learn so young and under such public circumstances. He was glad that his own kids couldn't see him now, looking like a nutcase on leave from the crazy house.

Whoever this Simple Simon asshole was, Mc-Clane wished he'd show his face. He was aching to take a poke at him, stick his gun between his eyes, and demand to know why he had chosen him. Why here in the middle of Harlem? And why this goddamn sandwich board that was smashing against his knees with every step he took?

He stepped onto the sidewalk and headed north toward the corner where 138th Street met Amsterdam Avenue, keeping his eyes peeled for any abrupt movements, any cars suddenly pulling onto the street, any sign of a terrorist with ten pounds of dynamite sticking out of his back pocket.

Halfway down the block, a door slammed shut. McClane automatically reached behind his back for his gun and swiveled to find the source of the noise. A stocky, middle-aged black woman stood for a moment on the stoop of a brownstone, checked the door to make sure it was locked, then turned and walked down the steps. He watched her expression, saw her mouth open in surprise as she approached him.

"What in heaven's name . . . ?" she exclaimed.

He nodded, acting as if the presence on a Harlem street of a half-naked white man wearing a sandwich board were an ordinary, everyday occurrence. "Morning, ma'am. I'm running for City Council. Hope I can count on your vote," he said, smiling politely.

The woman didn't say a word, but he could feel her staring after him as he passed her. His cop's instinct told him that she wasn't the only one to be following his progress as he continued on his way.

Zeus Carver spotted his nephews, Dexter and Raymond, through the window of his shop. They were moving slowly, looking very pleased with themselves, lugging an enormous boom box that had to weigh almost as much as the two of them put together. Zeus picked up his screwdriver and went back to working on the answering machine he'd promised to have fixed by four o'clock this afternoon. No need to go dashing out of the store when the boys were obviously coming to him.

Just what he needed: a busted boom box, most likely stolen or traded off of some crackhead. His shop was already crammed with enough broken refrigerators, dishwashers, washing machines, stereos, and TV sets to keep him busy into the next century. Mr. Zeus the Fix-It Man, as he was known in the neighborhood. With his light touch, he could have been a brain surgeon—if he'd been born with pink skin instead of the color of dark chocolate.

He was a genius at restoring life to ancient, battered electrical equipment that everyone else had given up for dead. It was a talent he'd discovered while still a kid, when he'd spent hours taking apart and reassembling watches, clocks, transistor radios . . . anything he could beg, borrow, or steal from his mother or the neighbors.

Just yesterday, he'd worked his magic on a TV that his landlord had found in an abandoned apartment. He had it on now, tuned to a news report about a bomb going off in some fancy downtown department store. The story interested him much less than the fact that he was getting a clear image and good sound, thanks to new picture tubes and a few other minor adjustments. He periodically glanced at the set, checking that the picture hadn't faded into a storm of black-and-white snow.

He caught glimpses of the wreckage, of the reporter droning on about the police department's lack of information regarding who might be responsible for the explosion. Just so they didn't blame it on a black man, he thought, as the front door buzzer rang. His nephews, panting from the strain of carrying the boom box, burst into the store. It took their combined efforts to lift the box up onto the counter.

"Uncle!" yelled eleven-year-old Dexter. Four years older than his brother, he was the ringleader of the pair, a wiry column of self-confident, exuberant energy who reminded Zeus of himself at that same age.

Zeus pointed to a clock on the wall. "It's ten after nine," he said. "Why aren't you in school?"

"Tony wants to sell you this," Dexter said, his voice rising with excitement.

Zeus scowled at him. "Tony? That no-neck dude they call 'Bad-T'?"

Raymond nodded. "He says he found it in a dumpster."

Sure. And black and white were equal in America. Raymond was a smart little boy, but he worshiped his older brother and was too damn innocent for his own good. "He keeps stealing things from people, they're gonna find him in a dumpster," said Zeus.

"No, he didn't steal this. He said his uncle gave it to him," Dexter declared, his eyes big and innocent as he contradicted his previous story.

"Uh-huh." Rather than point out the discrepancy, Zeus decided to take action. "Hand me that newspaper," he said.

Dexter obliged, then eagerly waited to hear his uncle's offer.

Zeus rolled up the paper and batted Dexter across the head, not quite hard enough to hurt him, but forcefully enough to make his point.

Dexter dodged away and bit his lip to keep from crying. He was more shocked than hurt by the blow. He was used to his mother hitting him, but not his Uncle Zeus.

"Don't ever let somebody use you," Zeus admonished the two boys. "You're hauling hot property all over town. If you get caught, you get in trouble, while Tony denies the whole thing and walks away."

He gazed sternly first at Dexter, then at Raymond, who looked even more stunned than his brother by Zeus's anger.

"You want us to take it back to Tony?" Raymond offered, eager to make amends with his favorite relative and surrogate father.

Zeus shook his head. "I'll take it back to Tony . . . with a message."

Raymond shivered. Tony was a trash-talking high school kid, who had a reputation around the neighborhood for being one tough dude. But his uncle was tougher. He pitied Tony and hoped Zeus wouldn't mess him up too badly.

"Where you going now?" Zeus asked.

They were used to his rapid-fire inquisition. All they had to do to earn his approval—and a couple of bucks if he was in a good mood—was to give him the answers he wanted as fast as he could ask the questions. It was kind of like learning the multiplication tables. If you got the drill right, didn't stumble over the eights and nines, the teacher awarded you with a smile and left you alone.

"School," said Raymond. He giggled with the relief of knowing they were moving on to more familiar territory.

"Why?" He glared at Dexter, signaling him to jump in.

Zeus was Dexter's hero, the person he most wanted to be like when he grew up. A lot of the other adults in his world seemed to have given up on life. Some of them smoked crack or pot or shot up as a way to ease their hurts and disappointments. Others drank away their sorrows. And there were those who were to be avoided because they were so cruel and quick to lash out with their fists.

Zeus was different. He didn't drink or do drugs. He stared people right in the eye when he spoke to them. He was tough but fair. He told you straight out if he liked something you'd done, let you know if he didn't.

"To get educated," Dexter said.

"Why?"

Raymond knew the answer to that one. "So we can go to college."

"Why's that important?"

"To get . . . 'espect." Raymond stumbled over the word.

"Re-spect," Zeus corrected him gently. "Who's the bad guys?"

"Guys who sell drugs," said Raymond.

"Guys who have guns," Dexter chimed in his two cents.

Zeus nodded. "That's right. Who's the good guys?"

Raymond pointed a chubby finger at himself, his brother, his uncle. "We're the good guys."

"Who's gonna help you?"

"Nobody," said Dexter.

Zeus frowned. He repeated the question, this time more loudly. "Who's gonna help you?"

"We're gonna help ourselves," said Raymond, his tone pitched somewhere between a question and an answer.

"And who do we not want to help us?"

"White people," Dexter said, redeeming himself.

"That's right," Zeus said solemnly. "Now get yourselves—"

He broke off mid-sentence, distracted by a sight so strange he had to move closer to the window to make sure he wasn't hallucinating.

He blinked and looked again. This was for real, not a figment of his imagination. A man . . . a WHITE man . . . was standing across the street from his shop, in the middle of the intersection of one of the worst streets in Harlem. He wasn't wearing much except a sandwich board that declared in huge red letters, I HATE EVERYBODY.

Take it downtown where it belongs, thought Zeus. Whitey could hate the whole damn human race, for all he cared. But not here, not across from his shop. The guy might as well be sending out engraved invitations to his own lynching. A crazy white man, hot weather, and a riot fit together like bacon, lettuce, and tomato. Zeus had put his whole life into his shop. He wasn't about to watch his future go up in flames because of some honky asshole.

"Dial 911," he instructed Dexter. "Tell them you want a police car up here fast—or somebody's gonna die."

Frightened by the urgency in his voice, the boys stood frozen.

"Move!" he shouted in his best drill-sergeant manner.

They ran for the phone as he hurried out the door, calling to them over his shoulder, "Then get your butts to school, hear me?"

He took a moment to assess the situation. Whitey appeared to be just standing around, not going anywhere any time soon. At the other end of the block was a group of neighborhood toughs, five or six young men in their late teens and early twenties. They were high school dropouts, exactly the kind of dudes he was raising his nephews not to be. Boys who thought they were men with too much time on their hands, who spent their days sprawled on the stoop, playing cards, drinking beer, and smoking dope.

They hadn't yet spotted Whitey. But it wouldn't be long before they'd tire of the card game or run out of beer, and go looking for some other way to amuse themselves. And when they did, there'd be trouble. Big trouble, and plenty of it.

He angled diagonally across the street to the intersection, feeling the heat closing in on the city like a wool blanket. With no shade to protect him from a relentless sun, Whitey would soon be broiled to a crisp . . . if the brothers didn't kill him first.

Ten feet away from the man, he stopped and stared at him quizzically. "Good morning," he said, keeping his voice even and friendly.

McClane glared at him and didn't say a word.

"Havin' a good day, sir? You feelin' okay?" Zeus asked. He edged closer, watching out for any sudden moves. Whitey looked calm enough, but you had to be careful with a nutcase like this.

"Not to get too personal, but a white man in the middle of Harlem wearing a sign that says he hates everybody has either got some serious personal issues, or not all of his dogs are barking," Zeus said.

McClane scowled at him but said nothing.

Zeus moved in a few more steps and lowered his voice. "I'm talkin' to you, man," he said angrily, trying to convey the urgency of his message. "You've got ten seconds before those guys see you. When they see you, they will kill you."

They were almost nose-to-nose, so close that Zeus could see the beads of sweat on the other man's forehead, the patches of stubble he'd missed shaving that morning. He could see the pulse beating slowly and steadily at the base of his neck, the man as relaxed as if he were spending the day at Jones Beach.

"Do you understand me?" he hissed. "You are about to have a *very bad day*!"

"Tell me about it," McClane said. A muscle jumped in his jaw. "I'm a cop."

"What?" Zeus squinted at him in disbelief.

"I can't explain. I'm on a case."

It was worse than Zeus had expected. "No! You *are* a case! Now go hide your ass in my store till the police get here." He glanced sideways and saw that the dudes were getting restless, as he'd known they would.

An argument had started. One of them, unhappy perhaps with the hand he'd been dealt, flung his cards in the air. The cards twirled like Frisbees, then fell to the curb a few yards away from the stoop. Another of the players cursed loudly and went to retrieve the cards. As he bent to grab them, he looked down the street.

His gaze locked on the white man in the sandwich board. "What the fuck?" he growled.

Zeus saw him motion to his friends, all of whom quickly shifted their attention from the card game to the intersection. "Aw, shit," he mumbled.

"Listen," McClane muttered, his speech clipped and urgent. "An hour ago somebody blew up Bonwit's."

"Yeah?"

"The asshole who did *that* said I had to do *this*. Or he'll blow up something else."

"What?" Under other circumstances, Zeus would have laughed out loud. He had to hand it to the guy. He had one hell of an imagination. For a white man.

The dudes had figured out something better to do with their morning than play cards. They were smiling and pointing as they strolled down the street. No need to hurry. Taking their time. The white man wasn't going anywhere any time soon . . . not with that crazy sign he was carrying.

"I've got a gun," McClane said quietly, knowing he'd be too outnumbered for a gun to do him much good.

"Where?" Zeus stared incredulously at him, then shook his head. "Never mind. You pull a gun, they'll kill you. Listen to me. You may not be crazy, but you're going to act crazy. Looney Toons. You read me?"

Impressed by the other man's quick thinking, McClane nodded. The plan was crazy, the kind of thing he might dream up to get himself out of a tight spot. It just might work. He'd been feeling kind of psychotic lately. It wouldn't be hard to come up with a convincingly wacky rap.

A moment later, the dudes had them surrounded, checking out the message on the sandwich board. They were amused. Sort of.

"Hey, Zeus. This a friend of yours?" asked the ringleader, a graduate of the Rikers Island prison who liked showing off what he could do with a knife.

Zeus forced his lips into a smile. "He look like a friend of mine? He's as crazy as your sister on a Saturday night."

He held his breath and prayed. His prayer was answered.

"Niagara Falls!" McClane shrieked, flapping his arms like a chicken gone wild. "Slowly I turn, step by step! I don't know—he's our shortstop! But I'm calm now! I'm much calmer than before! Just don't say . . . Niagara Falls! Slowly I turn, step by step . . ."

He turned, bared his teeth, and began stalking the man who had spoken to Zeus.

"He's drugged out or something. Stay away," Zeus advised the young man, who warily backed away.

McClane pretended to pick invisible bugs off his arms. "Her name was Sadie," he squawked. "But her sister called her Lou. I had to kill both of them . . . you can understand that. One of them breathed on me, but I didn't know which one."

He whirled around and shouted into the face of a second gang member, "So I had to kill them both!"

Startled, the man shot out his arm and popped a hard right to McClane's jaw. There was the sickening crunch of bone against bone. McClane wobbled from the impact of the punch but held his ground.

"That felt good." He grinned. "Please, sir, may I have another one?"

His assailant seemed happy to comply with another more powerful shot to the jaw. McClane spit blood from between his lips and reeled backwards, barely managing to stay on his feet.

Zeus winced. Crazy or not, this was one tough dude. A cop? Zeus didn't think so. What cop would keep on taking this kind of shit from a bunch of black men?

"That felt good," McClane said, the blood dribbling down his chin. "Insert another coin. If you need change, consult the vendor at the desk."

"Can't hurt the dude," declared his attacker, rubbing his knuckles.

"You can't hurt him because he's on Mars. Now leave him alone," Zeus said.

A third gang member pushed his way forward. "I can hurt him," he boasted. "Even on Mars."

He whipped out a switchblade, snapped it open, and shoved it under McClane's nose. That was all the encouragement his friends needed to join in the fun. One grabbed the front of the sandwich board, a second pulled at the back, a third slashed at the straps. The board clattered to the ground. The men hooted and cheered as they caught sight of McClane, exposed and vulnerable in his jockey shorts.

The man with the knife lunged at McClane's chest. But McClane was too quick for him and dodged out of range of the blade. As the young man thrust at him, again, Zeus spotted McClane's gun. Desperate to grab it before anyone else had the chance, he flung himself at McClane, ripped the gun away, and spun around to face the would-be assailants.

"Back off!" he yelled. "I don't want to, but I'll do it." He pointed the gun, training it left and right, imitating the cops he'd seen on TV.

His hands were shaking as he cocked the gun. He stepped backwards, closer to McClane.

The dudes had blood in their eyes. He'd betrayed them for a white man. They weren't going to give up without a fight. Didn't matter that he had the gun. They had the advantage of numbers—and the false courage that came from drinking malt liquor at nine A.M.

How long before they decided to jump him? And where the hell were the cops his nephews had called for?

He could hear Whitey next to him, breathing hard. He wanted to say, Man, do something. You got yourself into this. Now figure a way out. Then, as if by divine intervention, the way out appeared in the form of a livery cab that had braked to a stop at the red light.

Zeus spun around and aimed the gun at the windshield. The driver's face was a mask of terror. He could read the guy's mind. A black man with a gun was not his ideal passenger.

The light turned green.

"Stay where you are!" Zeus screamed at the driver.

With his free hand, he motioned McClane to get into the cab, then followed him, stepping backwards, the gun still pointed at the young men.

"Go!" he shouted.

The cabbie floored the gas pedal. The car roared through the intersection, and the gang chased it down the street, cursing Zeus, McClane, and both their families to the end of time. They let fly a volley of beer bottles, some of which hit the trunk with a dull thud, while others shattered against the half-open rear windows in a warm, sticky shower of beer and a spray of broken glass. They were doubling back, heading back towards his shop, when the cabbie suddenly turned around and thrust a wad of money under his nose.

His voice quavering with fear, the cabbie pleaded, "Don't kill me! That's all I got!"

Zeus pushed the man's hand away and shook his head. From the accent, he guessed the man was from one of the islands, most likely Jamaica. The poor slob was probably supporting a wife and kids in Kingston, and woke up every morning scared that this day would be his last on earth.

"Aw, man, I ain't robbin' you. Just get us outta here. Head downtown! Run the lights."

"You got it, boss," the driver said, sounding only slightly less terrified than before.

Who could blame him? One guy with a gun. The other one in his birthday suit. And both of them spattered with blood. Zeus touched his upper arm, came away with blood on his fingers, and realized he must have been cut by a piece of broken bottle.

"Is that deep?"

"No, just messy." Zeus stared at the man next to him, the white man for whom he'd risked his life and probably sacrificed his livelihood. The guy stunk of malt. The brothers must have been damn pissed to have wasted so much good beer on a honky. "So, one more time," he said, handing over the gun. "The guy who blew up Bonwit's sent you to Harlem wearing a sign saying 'I hate—' "

"Yep." McClane nodded. "Jesús, right?" he said, giving the name its Spanish pronunciation. "John McClane." He put out his hand. "I owe you. You'll be compensated for any loss of livelihood."

"Get your checkbook out because that was my appliance shop across the street," Zeus said sourly. "You have any idea what those guys are doing to it right now?"

McClane leaned back against the seat of the

cab and closed his eyes. His plans for the day had involved nothing more taxing than getting loaded and feeling sorry for himself. A street brawl with a bunch of Harlem punks hadn't exactly figured into the equation. His jaw was aching from the punches he'd taken, he smelled like he'd taken a Budweiser bubble bath, and he was dressed as if he were auditioning for a Calvin Klein ad. He didn't need anyone busting his chops just now.

"Chill out, Jesús. We'll have a car sent up," he said, gingerly touching the cut on the inside of his lower lip.

"Chill out?" Zeus glared at him. "What, are you trying to 'relate' to me? Speak like a white man. And where do you get off calling me 'Jesús'? Do I look Puerto Rican?"

McClane shrugged. He was only repeating what he'd heard on the street. "The guy back there called you 'Jesús,' " he tiredly explained.

"He didn't say 'Hey-zoos.' He said, 'Hey! Zeus!' My name is Zeus.

"Zeus." McClane sighed. Okay. Big fuckin' deal. No need to go ballistic. And what the hell kind of a name was that, anyhow?

"As in father of Apollo. Mount Olympus," Zeus informed him. "Don't-screw-with-me-or-I'll-shove-a-lightning-bolt-up-your-butt-Zeus. You have a problem with that?"

McClane smiled. He liked Zeus's "fuck-you" attitude, so similar to his own. Holly used to like that part of him, too, a long time ago. No more, though. Now, it was, Fuck you, John, and get out of my life. He sighed, wondering for the umpteenth time how things had gotten so screwed up between him and Holly, and said, ''You're a helluva date, Zeus.''

The driver peered at him through the rearview mirror. ''Where you boys headed?'' he asked suspiciously.

McClane imagined what the driver must be thinking and almost laughed out loud at the image: He had them pegged for a couple of gays—one of them mostly naked, the other one armed for action—out on a date. It would make a hell of a great New York story for the folks back home.

''Downtown. Police Plaza.''

''Shit,'' Zeus muttered, looking as if he would rather be any place else than where he was going.

Now what? McClane glanced at him sideways. How was it that most civilians never understood the police was there to protect them from the bad guys? Sure, cops misused their authority and things got a little rough sometimes in places like Harlem or Crown Heights. But prejudice against blacks or Hispanics didn't automatically come with the uniform, and McClane knew plenty of guys on the force who were color-blind.

Or maybe Zeus didn't like cops because he'd been arrested, maybe even done some time. He seemed like a straight enough guy, but then, so did some of the dirtiest cops McClane had ever met.

Either way, all he needed to do was give a quick statement, and then he was free to go.

McClane closed his eyes again, stopped speculating about Zeus's psyche, and tried to relax. The day was young, he was tired, and Simple Simon had yet to make his next move.

Chapter 3

McClane fell into a sound sleep and didn't wake up until the cab stopped in front of Police Plaza. The ache in his jaw had worsened, and he was desperate to take a piss because of all the coffee he drank on the way up to Harlem. He jumped out of the car, grabbed a uniform, and got him to take care of the fare. Then he hurried up the steps to the building, thinking that Zeus was right behind him.

Wrong. He stood on the sidewalk where he'd gotten out of the cab, gazing around as if he were trying to decide his next move. McClane motioned him to come inside. But Zeus shook his head.

McClane retraced his steps. "What's the problem?" he demanded.

Zeus kept on shaking his head. "No problem."

His cop's nose smelled a lie, but all he said was, "Then come on."

"I got no reason to go in there," Zeus said stubbornly.

Anybody else, McClane would have thought, the hell with it. But Zeus had saved his life, for Chrissakes.

"Sure you do. We tell the captain what happened, he'll give you a voucher to compensate for any damage to your shop, then you get a free ride home. C'mon," he said, and steered him through the door.

He left Zeus in the bullpen to give a statement and get his arm patched up, then went to check whether Simple Simon had been back in touch.

Cobb's office was a madhouse. A crew of technicians were swarming around and under his desk, hooking a tracer to the telephone wires. Lambert was crouched in a corner, digging through computer printouts to try and match Simon with a previous-arrest record. Adding to the confusion, Assistant Deputy Commissioner Phil Jordan was railing at Cobb about the need to observe proper lines of communication.

"Nobody called me!" He slammed his hand against the top of Cobb's desk. "Nobody asked me! There was no clearance from the mayor or me!"

Phil Jordan ranked among the top ten people

on earth McClane least wanted to run into right
now. Jordan was a tall, mean, political son of a
bitch, the kind of guy who would sell his grand-
mother if it would put him in line for another pro-
motion. McClane could forgive him for doing the
mayor's dirty work; *somebody* had to do it. But
he couldn't forgive how much Jordan enjoyed
doing the job.

He stuck around just long enough to hear Cobb
justify his decision to carry out Simon's instructions without consulting the mayor. Then he did
a quick about-face and went to find more coffee,
while Cobb wearily reiterated his position to Jordan. "There wasn't any time for clearance.
We've got a maniac out there."

This was hardly the first occasion—nor would
it be the last—that the chief of detectives would
have to eat shit for doing his job. He'd been
reamed out a thousand times before by men a lot
more ambitious and power-hungry than Jordan.
Absorbing the punishment for action taken in the
midst of crisis was all part of the job . . . a fine
point that the boys upstairs, who were more concerned with getting ahead than catching the bad
guys or protecting civilians, never seemed to
grasp.

"So you took this guy off probation, and now
we've got two maniacs out there!"

"Simon set a ticking bomb. He insisted on Mc-
Clane."

Jordan glared at Cobb. A vein in the middle of his forehead looked ready to burst. "He doesn't call the shots in this department. Neither does McWhatzisname, and neither do you!"

Cobb knew that if he'd waited to act until everyone met and agreed on a proper response to Simon's threat, the mayor could have had a full-scale crisis on his hands. Jordan ought to be kissing his ass right now instead of wasting both their time, carrying on like a spoiled kid. But what he knew, and what the mayor and his henchmen understood, were two altogether different stories. His was a no-win situation.

He met Jordan's angry gaze, but kept his mouth shut, knowing that Jordan had just about run out of steam. Sure enough, after a few moments of silence, Jordan stormed out of the office. He barely missed colliding with Fred Schiller, a departmental forensic psychologist who specialized in profiling terrorists. He had just begun to explain Simon's motivation when McClane, tipped off that the coast was clear, came strolling in, accompanied by an obliging secretary who'd volunteered to clean up the cut on his chin.

"It's about control, power, feeling omnipotent," Schiller was saying. He stroked his beard thoughtfully and gestured toward McClane. "He wants control over him, over his every move, over his thoughts, even his emotions."

McClane grimaced as the secretary soaked the

cut with hydrogen peroxide. "You're saying this guy's trying to send me flowers?"

Schiller shook his head. "Wrong emotion. This guy's ugly."

"How is it?" Cobb asked the secretary.

"Nothing wrong with him a shower wouldn't cure," she said. She carefully dabbed the wound with an antibiotic ointment, then smiled at Mc-Clane. "Beer is normally taken internally, John."

"I love you, too," he said, winking.

"This is Fred Schiller, John." Cobb said. "He's—"

"A shrink." McClane nodded. "I got it."

"I was saying that this guy's about power," Schiller went on. "He wants you to dance to his tune, he wants to pound you until you give up and then—"

"Kill me," McClane said flatly.

"Probably." Schiller agreed, just as matter-of-factly. "There'll be a huge amount of suppressed rage. It may show up physically when the guy's stressed."

"Is this somebody he arrested?" Cobb asked.

"We'll probably know soon enough. Megalo-maniacs don't act anonymously. He'll want you to know who's doing this. He's probably not using an alias. His name is Simon, or some variation."

"Bingo!" yelled Lambert, as if on cue. He gleefully brandished a sheet of paper. "Got a

Robert E. Simons. Busted in 'eighty-six. Extortion and kidnapping. Ten to fifteen, served seven for good behavior. He was released on a state work-furlough two months ago.''

"Check it," Cobb told Lambert.

Walsh walked into the office and tossed McClane the clothes he'd left behind in the van when he'd stripped down to his shorts.

"Thanks, Ricky," McClane said, pulling on the shirt.

He hated to burst Cobb's balloon, but there was no point in Lambert going off on a wild-goose chase. "You're wasting your time," he told Cobb. "Bob Simons was a bankrupt businessman who kidnapped his partner's daughter. He's a fuck-up, not a psycho. The guy we're dealing with is nuts."

"A nut who knows a lot about bombs," Charlie Weiss chimed in, before Cobb had a chance to debate the point with McClane.

Weiss, the head of the bomb squad, stood in the doorway, brandishing an ordinary-looking leather briefcase, distinguished only by the antenna that protruded between the top and bottom halves of the case. He squeezed himself into the already crowded office and slapped down the briefcase onto Cobb's desk.

"They found this in a playground. Professional," he said admiringly. "Very cool stuff.

You know . . ." He threw his arms into the air and loudly simulated an explosion. *"Boom!"*

Cobb edged away from the case. "Should you slam it around like that?" he asked.

Weiss popped open the briefcase. It contained a specially fitted rack of small glass tubes, filled almost to the top with either red or clear-colored liquid. "It's unmixed. You can't hurt it," he assured Cobb.

Weiss was a smart, no-nonsense guy who had an encyclopedic knowledge of explosive devices and was missing the ends of two fingers from a partially deactivated grenade that had gone off too soon. McClane had a lot of respect for him and the rest of his bomb squad team. At one point, he'd even considered asking to be transferred over there. But the job required absolutely steady hands, and he'd figured the work might interfere with his drinking.

"This stuff's cutting edge," Weiss said. "It's a *binary liquid.*"

Cobb wrinkled his brow. "A what?"

"Like epoxy. Two liquids. Look . . ." Uncorking two of the tubes, he first spilled a drop of the red liquid onto the desk, then next to it an equal amount of the clear liquid. He pulled off a shoe and hammered it onto the two pools of liquid.

"Either one, by itself, you got nothing. But mix them . . ."

He picked up a paperclip and straightened it

out. He combined a minute amount of both liquids on the end of the clip. Then he took aim and threw the clip into the bullpen. There was a loud blast. A chair exploded in a burst of flames.

Someone grabbed the fire extinguisher and sprayed it at the chair. A couple of other men beat down the flames with whatever came to hand.

"Christ Almighty, Charlie!" Cobb exclaimed. Stunned by the graphic demonstration, he stared at the wrecked, still-smoldering chair.

The bomb squad chief grinned. "Very cool stuff. With a package like this, you get a warning. The bomb has to arm. You'll see the red liquid pump into the clear before it detonates."

"How *long* before?" asked McClane.

Weiss shrugged. "Ten seconds, two minutes, could be anything. But once it's mixed?" He grinned again. "Be somewhere else."

"This stuff has gotta be pretty rare," said Cobb. "We should be able to—"

"We already did," Lambert broke in. He tore off a sheet of computer printout and handed it to Cobb. "Livermore Labs, theft over the weekend."

"Has he got enough to make another?" McClane asked.

"Enough?" Lambert raised an eyebrow. "They think they lost close to a ton."

Cobb pointed at the drops on his desk and scowled. "Of that?"

McClane was suddenly very, very thirsty. It was just about the time he usually started in on the scotch, just to get the day off to a proper start. He saw the fear in Cobb's eyes, saw Lambert's mouth tighten with anxiety, and wondered whether his own eyes mirrored their tension.

There wasn't much that scared him, except perhaps the thought of never seeing his kids again or hearing from Holly that she'd fallen in love with another man. Legally, they were still married, and he figured that as long as she hadn't met someone else, they still had a chance to get back together. Trouble was, on those increasingly rare occasions when they spoke on the phone, they'd inevitably get into the same old, tired arguments that always ended with one of them hanging up on the other.

She wanted him to stop drinking, come back to LA, quit being a cop, get some kind of cushy desk job. Her bosses at the Nakatomi Corporation were deeply grateful to him for saving the lives of so many of their employees that terrible Christmas Eve. All she had to do was ask, and they'd find work for him in one of their many subsidiaries.

He couldn't see it. He'd moved out there for awhile, joined the LAPD, made a real effort to be the play-it-safe kind of guy that Holly wanted. But he was a goddamn *cop*, for Chrissakes, not a pencil pusher. And LA was too damn hot and sunny for his tastes. A nice place to visit, maybe, like Disneyland or Las Vegas. But live there? No thanks. No way.

New York was in his blood. He liked waking up to the sounds of horns blaring and people screaming and garbage trucks screeching in the street below his window. He liked the feel of Times Square at midnight: the whores strutting their stuff, the hustlers playing three-card monte, the neon peep show signs lighting up the darkness with lurid promises of titillation. He even liked riding the subways at all hours of the day or night, leaning against a steel pole and watching his fellow New Yorkers through half-closed eyes, mentally daring the punks to play into his hands by starting a fight with one of the other passengers.

New York was his town. Leaving it would be like giving up on Holly and his marriage. It might not be working the way it was supposed to be, but it was all he had.

He wasn't especially scared of death. He'd stared into the face of danger and walked away laughing so often that he figured he'd stay alive until the moment he was meant to die. But he resented like hell the idea of being toyed with by a crazy man with a ton of liquid explosives at his disposal.

"The detonating mechanism can be anything," Weiss said as if he were teaching a high-school chemistry class. "Radio, electrical . . . hell, you could use a beeper and phone it in."

As Weiss continued his lecture on the effectiveness of binary liquids, McClane saw Cobb's secretary signaling to get her boss's attention.

"It's him," he heard Jane tell Cobb.

"This one has a doubled Alberti feedback loop," Weiss went on, so caught up in his excitement over the ingenuity of Simon's device that he failed to pick up on the tension in Jane's voice. "It's a nasty little trick I believe was first used in Lebanon by the—"

"Charlie." Cobb tried to interrupt the flow of information. *"Charlie!"*

Weiss stopped mid-syllable, noticed Cobb pointing to the phone, and finally shut up.

"Start the trace," Cobb ordered Walsh.

He nodded at Jane to put the call through to his office. The phone buzzed. Cobb hit the RECORD button on his tape deck. McClane, Lambert, and Schiller grabbed for headsets. Cobb waited until they were all plugged in, then picked up the receiver.

"Simon?" he said.

"He wore the board. Walked the street. And survived," Simon intoned, speaking as if he were reciting lines from a children's poem. He said a few words in what McClane guessed to be German, then switched back to English. "Who would have guessed? Where are my pigeons now?''

Confused, Cobb looked at Schiller, who shook his head. ''Pigeons?'' Cobb asked.

'' 'I had two pigeons, bright and gay, / Fly from me the other day. / Why was it they did go? / You cannot tell. You do not know.' ''

''You mean McClane,'' said Cobb.

''No. Santa Claus.''

Cobb glanced at Schiller, looking for input as to how to proceed. Schiller nodded at McClane to jump into the conversation.

''I'm here,'' McClane said into his mouth-piece.

''Ah. There after all.''

Simon's voice, with its thick accent and mock-ing tone, was getting on McClane's nerves. This Simon, whoever he was, was altogether too damn pleased with himself. And why shouldn't he be? He had the cops waiting on his every word, run-ning around the city taking his orders. Yeah, they were pigeons all right . . . as in a pathetic bunch of easy marks, taken in by his threats.

''And the other one?'' Simon asked.

Cobb snapped his fingers at McClane. Who the hell was the other one? McClane pointed at Zeus, who appeared to be negotiating with one of the other detectives for a quick ride back to Harlem.

''Yeah. He's here, too,'' said McClane, as Lambert darted out of the room, grabbed Zeus, and pulled him into the office. Meanwhile Cobb put the call on the speakerphone.

"Well, put the ebony Samaritan on," ordered Simon.

Zeus stiffened. "You got a problem with ebony?" he demanded.

McClane held his breath. This was not a good moment for Zeus to launch into a tirade about racism and black pride. They needed to keep Simon talking long enough to trace the call. Pissing him off could only complicate matters.

But Simon didn't seem to mind Zeus's hostility. "Oh, hello," he said. "No, my only problem is that I went to some trouble preparing that game for McClane. You interfered with a well-laid plan."

"Yeah? Well, you can stick your well-laid plan up your well-laid ass," Zeus shouted into the speakerphone.

Simon's patience had run out. McClane heard a sharp click, followed by a dial tone. Zeus had blown it. Simon was gone. The line was dead.

Cobb slammed down the phone. "That was *not smart!*" he bellowed at Zeus. "There are lives at stake!"

The crowded office suddenly became very still and close, as if all the oxygen had been sucked out of the atmosphere. The mere act of breathing seemed to take extra effort. They were all seasoned cops, used to dealing with crime in all its various manifestations. But having a civilian in their midst put a different face on things. Zeus was an outsider, drawn against his will into a life-and-death drama that required particular training and talents. Watching him screw up was a reminder of their own fears and weaknesses.

McClane could feel Zeus's tension, his resistance to getting involved in a police matter. He was simmering with resentment about to boil over . . . and there was something else there, as well. Something that McClane had sensed earlier, when Zeus had put up a fuss about coming down to headquarters.

"You'd better hope he calls back," Cobb growled at Zeus.

"He will," Schiller reassured him.

Cobb opened his mouth, thought twice about whatever he'd been about to say, and shut it. There was a long, dreadful minute of silence. The men stared at the phone, willing it to ring. Willing Simon to resurface so they could find him and stop him before he did any more damage.

It did ring again, as Schiller had predicted. Cobb grabbed the receiver and said immediately, "Simon? He wasn't speaking for us."

"That was unpleasant," Simon said, his voice low and menacing. "Don't let it happen again. What's your name, boy?"

McClane groaned inwardly. Whether by design or accident, Simon had twice managed to hit

Zeus's most sensitive area. Cobb waved a warning finger at Zeus to keep his mouth shut. Too late.

"Don't call me 'boy,' " Zeus shot back. He glared at the other men, as if daring them to disagree.

Simon surprised them by not hanging up. "Sorry. A poor attempt at humor." He chuckled, a dry, hollow rattle that made McClane think of a bleak winter wind on a bitter January night. "I was going to send you home with a chiding," said Simon. "But now I think perhaps you'll join the game."

Before Zeus had a chance to respond, Walsh snapped his fingers to grab their attention. "We got him!" he whispered, pointing to the tracer. "Pay phone in . . ." He waited an agonizing second for the technician at the other end of his headset to give him the area code. Then he said, "Oslo?"

Brooklyn or Queens would have been enough of a surprise. Oslo made no sense whatsoever.

"Norway?" Cobb echoed Walsh's shock.

Walsh shook his head. "Wait! It's Juarez, Mexico." He frowned, as the technician updated him. "Shit! Now they think it's Australia—"

Simon was a real pro. Your average small-time crook had no idea how to reroute calls through the international circuits. It took a special kind of genius to set up a system that could outwit NYPD's ultrasophisticated tracing equipment.

"So much for a trace," McClane said glumly. He wondered what other talents Simon still had hidden up his sleeve, besides being an explosives experts and a high-tech phone wiz?

"Having fun with the phone company, are we?" Simon laughed, sounding like a child relishing a brand-new toy. But his voice quickly turned low and ugly. "Simon says McClane and the Samaritan go to the subway station at Seventy-second and Broadway. I will call you in fifteen minutes on the pay phone outside the station. No police. Failure to answer will constitute noncompliance. Do you understand me, John?"

"Not one bit," McClane said, barely concealing his irritation.

He wanted to ask Simon where the hell he got off calling him "John"? In fact, where did he get off calling him anything at all? He didn't need this kind of crap.

Though it was only the middle of June, the weatherman had predicted a real scorcher, with high humidity and record temperatures. Not the kind of day, under the best of circumstances, that McClane felt like hanging around on various street corners, waiting to hear from some asshole with a grudge. And these weren't the best of circumstances, in case anyone was interested, which didn't seem to be the case.

"Seems to me," he said, shooting a quick glance at Schiller, "you're just some psycho who likes to play kids' games."

The words were out of his mouth before he saw Schiller wince and vigorously shake his head. No! No! Wrong approach!

McClane waited for the click that would mean Simon had hung up on him.

But this time, Simon stayed on the line. "Hardly!" he said angrily.

McClane decided to push his luck and press him further. "Let me guess. I sent you up for something. Shoplifting, female impersonation . . ."

"You? You couldn't catch me if I stole your chair with you in it!" Simon sputtered.

Screw the bastard, and screw trying to keep his cool. "Then why are you trying to kill me, asshole?" he snapped.

"John, calm yourself," Simon chided him. "If killing you was *all* I wanted, you'd be dead by now." He laughed again, another blast of winter wind that McClane felt in his bones.

"Simon, this is Cobb," the chief broke in. "I appreciate your feelings about McClane, but believe me, the jerk isn't worth it."

McClane threw him a dirty look: *Thanks for the support, boss.*

Cobb ignored him and went on talking to Simon as if McClane weren't in the room. "He's stepped on so many toes in the department that this time next month he'll be a security guard. His own wife wants nothing to do with him. And he's maybe two steps shy of being an alcoholic. Why waste your time? Look, you sound like a smart guy. What would it take to call this off?''

"You mean . . . money.''

"Yeah. McClane's a toilet-bug,'' Cobb said, much too sincerely to suit McClane. "How about, say, a million bucks in unmarked bills to forget him and live happily ever after?''

"Money is shit to me. I would not give up Mc-Clane for all the gold in your Fort Knox.''

Schiller scribbled notes on his pad. Such contempt. Such a sense of conviction. The man had responded to the offer of a payoff just as Schiller would have expected him to.

Simon repeated the instructions. "Seventy-second Street subway. Pay phone. Fifteen minutes. McClane and the Samaritan. If you're competent in the least, you've found the briefcase. So you know what I mean by 'penalty.' ''

He hung up before Cobb had a chance to make a second offer.

"Thank you, Walter,'' said McClane. "You were so supportive.''

"It was worth a try.'' Cobb shrugged, then turned to Schiller, as if for confirmation. "He's a raving maniac.''

Schiller nodded his agreement. "Textbook megalomania. Couldn't be clearer if you took it from a case study." He stroked his beard as he consulted his notes. "He gave clues to his identity. Spoke German, called it 'your' Fort Knox. And he stammered when McClane pushed him."

In other words, he was foreign-born. McClane didn't need a Ph.D. in psychology to figure that one out.

"You believe he really can't be bought off?" Cobb asked.

"Not a chance. From the textbook. The suggestion of money only increased his rage," said Schiller.

Cobb sighed. He was not a happy man. He opened his drawer, pulled out McClane's shield, and tossed it over to him.

The gold shield landed a couple of inches short of McClane's hand. He itched to reach for it, to stick it back in his pocket where it belonged. But he wasn't about to make it so easy on his boss. He hadn't forgiven him yet for the toilet-bug crack.

"You asking me to be a cop again, Walter?" he asked.

Cobb reached for his antacid pills. "You two better get going if you're going to make Seventy-second in time," he said, avoiding a direct answer to McClane's question. "Walsh, flag them a cab."

"Whoa, hold on!" Zeus declared.

The cops all looked over at him.

"I'm not going anywhere," he announced.

"Simon says you have to," Cobb reminded him.

Like Zeus could give a rat's ass, thought McClane. Cobb seemed to have forgotten that Zeus wasn't on the payroll.

"I'm not jumping through hoops for some psycho," Zeus calmly informed them. "That's a white man with white problems. You deal with him. I was a fool to get messed up in this in the first place."

He turned and headed out of Cobb's office.

In theory, McClane had to agree with him. But he needed Zeus to come along, to make Simon believe they were playing his game. No matter what, he couldn't let Zeus off the hook until he had Simon safely locked away.

"Why'd you save my butt?" McClane blurted out the first thing that came into his head.

Zeus turned and glared at him. "I didn't! I stopped a white cop from getting killed in Harlem! One white cop gets killed in Harlem, and next day we have a thousand white cops—and every one of 'em with an itchy trigger finger. Got it?"

He stormed out, leaving behind a roomful of cops, silenced by the knowledge that he wasn't very far from the truth.

Cobb was the first the break the silence. "Get him back, John," he said.

"Where'd you find that bomb?" McClane asked Weiss.

"Chinatown."

"Shit." It wasn't the answer McClane had been hoping to hear. He didn't have much to work with, so he decided to improvise. He picked up his shield, feigning an air of total nonchalance, and hurried after Zeus.

"Wait up, partner," he called.

"I ain't your partner. I ain't your brother, your neighbor, or your friend. I am your total stranger," Zeus retorted over his shoulder.

McClane got the picture. "All right. Stranger." He raised his voice. "You know where the playground at 109th and St. Nicholas is?"

Zeus stopped and turned around. "It's in Harlem."

From his tone of weary resignation, McClane sensed Zeus had already figured out where their conversation was headed.

"Where do you think he put that briefcase?"

He paused for a second, to give Zeus a chance to shape the image in his mind: a playground crowded with little black kids; an innocent-looking briefcase filled with test tubes that no right-minded child could resist turning into a science experiment; an explosion that would instantly transform those kids into randomly arranged piles of body parts.

He said, "This guy doesn't care about skin color, even if you do."

Zeus straddled the doorway. His expression told McClane that he'd hit upon the one argument that could persuade Zeus to take a ride with him uptown.

McClane suddenly thought back to the first and last fishing trip he'd been talked into by a buddy years earlier. His friend had showed him how to bait the hook and cast his rod off the side of the boat into the placid lake waters. After an hour or two spent lazing in the sun and drinking beer, he'd felt a sharp tug on his line. Without too much effort, he'd reeled in a nice-sized perch that had tasted delicious when they grilled it for dinner.

A pleasant enough experience—but not one he'd ever cared to repeat. The odds of catching that fish had been weighted too heavily in his favor. Now, he'd hooked Zeus with an easy lie, and he was dragging him into a potentially dangerous situation. It didn't feel right. But did he have a choice?

Simon said no.

Chapter 4

The first thing McClane noticed when the cab driver hit the corner of Broadway and Seventy-second was the potent, garlic-scented aroma wafting out of Gray's Papaya. His mouth watered just thinking about their famous grilled hot dogs, two for a buck, slathered with mustard, ketchup, and relish. All he'd had for breakfast was coffee, cigarettes, and plenty of aggravation. No wonder he was hungry. The guys behind the counter worked fast. It wouldn't take more than a minute to grab a couple of dogs and a drink.

He scrambled out of the cab and checked the computerized time and temperature sign at the top of the bank across the street. It was almost nine forty-five. Cobb would rip off his head and make sure he was kicked off the force if he screwed up over a couple of hot dogs. The guy had a bad stomach. He couldn't appreciate the finer things in life.

The subway station entrance was located on a triangular island at the point where Broadway intersected Amsterdam Avenue and veered westward. The building that housed the token booths and turnstiles was a squat, old-fashioned, brick structure which fronted on Seventy-second Street. The newsstand was on the west side of the station; next to it was the pay phone that Simon had specified.

McClane stepped into the intersection as the amber light turned red and motioned to Zeus to follow him. A northbound truck barreled toward him. He ignored the warning honk and kept walking across the street. A taxi swerved out of his path and barely missed hitting Zeus.

"First time in my life I help some white guy, and look what it gets me," Zeus complained, dodging the oncoming traffic.

McClane didn't want to hear about it. "Hey, I was in the middle of a comfortable suspension, drinking scotch with Thunderbird chasers, smoking five packs of cigarettes a day," he told Zeus. "Suddenly, my life had meaning. Then . . . this."

He glanced at the phone and realized that Simon had overlooked one thing when he'd laid out his instructions. The Upper West Side was one of the city's most densely populated areas. If you were lucky enough to find a working pay phone, chances were better than even that somebody else had found it first.

A large, dark-haired woman with several bags of groceries at her feet stood clutching the telephone as if it were her lifeline to salvation. Sweat beaded her forehead and coursed down her cheeks as she spoke into the receiver in a low, urgent tone. McClane tapped his foot and glanced impatiently at his watch. Two minutes to go. A unending torrent of words tumbled out of the woman's mouth. She gave no sign of noticing McClane nor of finishing her conversation any time soon.

Lambert, Walsh, and Kowalski were positioned inside an unmarked police van parked diagonally across from the subway entrance. Lambert sat crouched over the two-way transmitter, giving Cobb a play-by-play of the action.

"They're at the phone, but there's a problem," he told Cobb.

"How big a problem?"

"About three hundred pounds." Lambert quoted Walsh, who sat sprawled in the driver's seat, pretending to nap while he kept a close watch on McClane.

He heard Cobb swear under his breath as he chewed on his antacid pills. It could be over before it began . . . all because the fat lady wouldn't stop singing.

* * *

McClane saw the van and knew his pals were keeping Cobb updated. He hoped that Cobb could pacify Simon if he called in to complain that he couldn't get through on the pay phone. Very casually, he glanced at the streets adjacent to the island. He wondered whether Simon was nearby, within sighting distance.

Directly across the street was a tiny slice of green named Verdi Park. During the seventies, long before the neighborhood had undergone its rebirth and real estate values had soared, the site had been nicknamed Needle Park. A magnet for drug dealers, the site had virtually functioned as an open-air supermarket for anything that could be smoked, snorted, or shot up. The cops and the community had worked together to banish the dealers and their clientele. But according to McClane's undercover friends, the benches facing Amsterdam Avenue were still frequented by small-time pushers mumbling whispered offers of crack and dope to unsuspecting passersby, and the whole area was a favorite target of pickpockets.

It was easy to see why. The sidewalks were clotted with pedestrians. Platoons of nannies, walking two and three abreast, pushed their tiny charges in strollers that left no room for the workbound yuppies who were recent additions to the neighborhood. Actors, actual and aspiring, strolled by, trading gossip about who was screwing whom on and off-Broadway. Graceful young women with necks like swans and turned-out feet hurried to their ballet classes at nearby Lincoln Center. Harried middle-aged women laden with shopping bags filled with bagels and lox and pesto and sun-dried tomatoes from Zabar's or Fairway groped in their pockets for change for the legions of homeless who'd taken up permanent residence in the neighborhood.

A train rumbled into the station below. The screech of its brakes, audible through the ventilation grates even above the bustle of street traffic, was a clamorous reminder that the seconds to blast-off were quickly counting down.

A couple with two children, all of them casually dressed in T-shirts, shorts, and sandals, stopped a few feet away to consult a subway map. The woman flashed a gap-toothed smile at McClane as her husband struggled to read the map. The little girl tugged at her mother's arm. "Not now, Sarah," said the woman. "Mummy's too tired and hot."

Tourists. Any minute now they'd be asking him how to get to the Statue of Liberty. He deliberately turned his back to them and looked at his watch. It was time for Mama Cass to say goodbye.

He tapped her on the shoulder. "Excuse me, ma'am," he said politely. "We need to use—"

"Get off the damned phone, lady!" Zeus stepped between the two of them, stuck out his arm, and broke the connection. "This is police business!"

The woman gaped at them. Her mouth opened wide, but no sounds came out. She gulped, grabbed her bags, and moved away from them as quickly as she could manage.

Zeus grinned at McClane. "I could get used to this," he said.

"There's another phone across the street, ma'am," McClane shouted after the woman. He whirled back around to take care of Zeus. "Let's get something straight," he said, gritting his teeth. "*I'm* on police business. You're not."

Zeus's grin faded fast. "You get something straight," he said, jabbing his index finger into McClane's chest. "You need me more than I need you. You don't like the way I do things . . . fine. I quit."

He got as far as the door to the station when the telephone rang. He stopped and turned to stare defiantly at McClane.

McClane was torn between wanting to grab the phone and tell Simon to go screw himself, and wanting to give Zeus the same message. Under the circumstances, neither choice made much sense. "All right. I need you," he grudgingly admitted.

Zeus held his ground. This was a rare opportunity, possibly once in a lifetime, a chance to lord it over a white cop.

McClane sighed. Zeus had him by the balls. "All right. I need you more than you need me."

Satisfied that he'd scored his point, Zeus sauntered back as McClane grabbed the receiver and said, "Yeah?"

Zeus huddled next to him, both of them listening for Simon's next set of orders.

But first he had to subject them to another of his Mother Goose poems. "Birds of a feather flock together, / So do pigs and swine. / Rats and mice have their chance, / As will I . . . have mine."

"Nice. It rhymes," said McClane, wishing Simon would get to the point of his call so they could end the scavenger hunt and stop playing games.

"Why was the phone busy? Who were you calling?" he demanded.

"The Psychic Hotline," McClane snapped.

"I'd advise you to take this more seriously."

McClane shrugged. The guy had no sense of humor. "Look, it's a public phone, what can I say?"

"You can simply say there was a fat woman on it, and it took you a minute to get her off."

So the cops weren't the only ones who were keeping an eye on him. McClane scanned the surrounding buildings. A modern high-rise dominated the immediate skyline, its brick facade broken by hundreds of windows that faced the subway station. Simon could be standing at any one of them, watching him through a pair of high-power binoculars, plotting his next move.

"There's a significant amount of explosive—in the trash receptacle next to you."

The very same trash receptacle against which Zeus had been leaning. He jumped away with a yelp of alarm.

"Try to run, and it goes up now," Simon warned.

The bastard! "I'm not going to, but there's a hundred people out here!" McClane said, glancing from the wire receptacle to the throngs of people walking in and out of the station.

"That's the point," said Simon, sounding amused. "Now pay attention," he went on, and began talking very quickly. "As I was going to St. Ives, / I met a man with seven wives. / Every wife had seven sacks, / Every sack had seven cats. / Every cat had seven kittens. Kittens, cats, sacks, and wives . . . , How many were going to St. Ives?"

The words spilled out so rapidly that by the time Simon got to the last line McClane could barely remember the beginning. "Whoa, wait!" he said. "Do it again."

"Not a chance. My phone is 555 and the answer. Call me in thirty seconds or die."

Click. He was gone.

McClane stared at Zeus. "We're dead."

"Shut up! I'm good at this stuff," said Zeus.

That made one of them. He'd never been any good at riddles, not even as a kid. Murderers and thieves, arsonists and drug dealers . . . those he could handle, easy. He was totally out of his depth here. And the precious seconds were ticking away, the moment of mass murder fast approaching. He racked his brain, trying to remember the rhyme.

"Seven women with seven bags of shit or something—"

"Shut the fuck up, McClane!" shouted Zeus, computing the numbers faster than a street-corner bookie. "Seven wives with seven sacks is forty-nine sacks. What was the rest?"

"I don't know! Cats and kittens!"

"Right, right, good! Seven cats, seven kittens. Forty-nine times seven is three hundred and . . . forty-three. Right?"

"What the hell you asking me for?"

"Three forty-three times seven is, hold on . . ." Zeus drew numbers in the air with his index finger. "Two times seven, carry one, times forty, add the two . . ."

McClane forgot to breathe. They were running out of time. Hurry! Get it! he silently urged Zeus.

". . . and you got two thousand four hundred and one," Zeus declared with a whoosh of relief.

McClane let out his breath. "Yeah, that's what I've got. Two-four-oh-one?" he asked, just to make sure.

Zeus nodded. "Dial five-five-five-two-four-oh-one."

"Five-five-five-two-four-oh-one." McClane repeated the numbers aloud as he dialed.

"No, wait! Wait!" Zeus grabbed the receiver out of his hand and disconnected the line. "It's a trick! I forgot the man!"

Was he nuts? Frantic now, McClane screamed, "Fuck the man! What number do I dial?"

"How many are going to St. Ives, right?" Zeus pounded his palm against his forehead and said, "The riddle starts, 'As *I* was going to St. Ives, I *met* a man with seven wives.' The guy and his wives aren't going anywhere!"

"Then *what* are they doing?"

"Sitting in the fucking road! Going in the other direction!" Zeus shouted. "How the fuck should I know?"

Any moment now, the bomb would blow, taking half the Upper West Side with it, and McClane was stuck in the middle of an Abbot and Costello routine with a black man named Zeus. "Then who's going to St. Ives?" he yelled.

"The guy! The guy telling the riddle! The answer is one!" Zeus thrust the receiver at him. "Call!"

McClane didn't follow the logic but decided to

take his word for it and ask questions later . . . *if*
there was a later. He pressed the first three numbers, then stopped abruptly. "Five-five-five-one?
How do I dial one?"

"Five-five-five-zero-zero-zero-zero-one!"
Zeus spelled it out for him. "Hurry the fuck up!"

His heart was pounding as he punched in the
last four numbers. The phone rang once. *Please!*
he prayed. *Let it be—*

"Hello, John," Simon sang out.

He telegraphed a silent thank you to Zeus, who
smirked in triumph. "Piece of cake," he said, as
his heartbeat gradually slowed to its normal rate.
"Next time, give us a hard one."

"But you're ten seconds late. Boom."

McClane grabbed Zeus and dived to the sidewalk, trying to put as much distance as possible
between himself and the receptacle. "There's a
bomb in the trashcan!" he screamed as he hit the
ground.

He covered his head with his arms and waited.
A second passed, another, then a third. He looked
up. People were staring at him and Zeus as they
walked by. He knew what they were thinking: just
a couple of typical New York crazies. The streets
were full of them. It took a lot to shock New
Yorkers. Two men hugging a patch of concrete
and carrying on about a bomb was nowhere near
a good enough reason to be late for work.

McClane sighed and picked himself up off the

sidewalk. He glanced at the surveillance van and wondered whether Lambert and the others had appreciated his performance. Or Simon, for that matter. Simon . . .

The phone receiver was dangling from the cord. He could hear Simon chuckling as he picked it up and muttered, "Yeah?"

"Didn't say, 'Simon says . . . ,' " the terrorist chortled.

McClane clenched his jaw to keep from responding as he would have liked to. The bomb might still be planted in the trashcan. He didn't want to give Simon a good excuse to set it off.

"It's 9:50. The Number Three train will arrive any second," Simon informed him.

McClane craned his neck around the corner of the building to peer through the ventilation grate. The platforms were crowded with commuters. A train was pulling in on the express track, right on schedule.

"I left something provocative on that train, John. Simon says get to the pay phone next to the news kiosk in the Wall Street station by 10:20 or the Number Three train and its passengers vaporize. Use any means of travel other than civilian, I blow the train. Attempt to evacuate the subway, I blow the train. I'll call in thirty minutes. Be there. Toodle-loo."

Click. He was gone.

The dial tone hummed in McClane's ear.

Think! he told himself. Who was this guy? What did he really want? He squinted into the sun, trying to put himself in Simon's place. Where was be calling from? It had to be somewhere nearby . . . or maybe not.

Simon had obviously carefully researched every detail of his high-stakes scavenger hunt. He'd even figured out the subway schedule, which was more than most daily commuters had ever done. It figured he wasn't working alone. He had to have an accomplice—possibly a whole team of them—reporting in while he sat back, called the shots, and enjoyed the show.

"Ninety blocks in thirty minutes in morning rush? Could be double that. And we don't even have a car!" Zeus neatly summed up their current predicament.

Simon had brought them halfway up the length of Manhattan in order to send them all the way back downtown. This made twice now that he had set up McClane for a possible hit, then spared him. Whatever his game was, he wanted McClane to keep on playing it with him. He had to be counting on the possibility that McClane might conceivably catch up with the southbound train. There was only one way to get to Wall Street.

"Taxi!"

McClane vaulted over the waist-high, protective steel fence that surrounded the subway station island. He flashed his shield at an empty cab that was stopped at the traffic signal. "Police officer!" he screamed through the window. "I'm requisitioning this vehicle for police business, sir!"

The driver stared at McClane in shocked silence, then desperately shook his head no. The traffic up ahead was starting to move. McClane figured maybe the guy didn't understand English. He yanked open the door and hauled the protesting driver out of the car. Zeus, meanwhile, had already dashed around to the passenger side and jumped into the front seat.

"Your police department appreciates it. Have a nice day!" McClane yelled at the driver, who was shaking his fist and shouted in a foreign language as he drove off.

"Pretty slick. Show a badge, get a car," said Zeus. "Listen, I used to drive a cab, and—"

McClane pressed hard on the gas. He swung the car into a U-turn that sent them skidding across Broadway and through the intersection.

"What were you saying?" he asked, as he ran the red light and zoomed east on Seventy-second Street.

"I was saying I used to drive a cab and Ninth Avenue is the fastest way south. But we seem to be headed east," Zeus said softly, grabbling for his seat belt.

McClane glanced through the rearview mirror. The surveillance van had backed into Seventy-

second Street and fallen into line a few cars behind him. He ignored the red light at Columbus
Avenue and almost got broadsided on the passenger side by a crosstown bus that was pulling away
from the stop.

The bus driver leaned heavily on his horn, and
Zeus let go a blood-curdling cry. "Where the hell
are you going, McClane?" he cried. "I'm telling
you Ninth Avenue is the quickest way south!"

"I know what I'm doing," he calmly assured
Zeus, as the speedometer soared past eighty.

"Even God doesn't know what you're doing!"
Zeus said, gritting his teeth. "We're heading
east!"

"I know."

"Wall Street is south!"

"Don't yell at me," McClane said. Then he
relented. For the time being, they were stuck with
each other. McClane hadn't had much luck with
partners. But hell, his luck could change, and
Zeus was doing his best to be helpful. The guy
hadn't volunteered for this particular tour of duty,
he'd been drafted. Why not give him a break?

He grinned at Zeus and said, "The best way
south isn't Ninth Avenue, it's through the park."

He swerved to avoid hitting a bunch of Japa-
nese tourists, headed for a photo-shoot in front of
the Dakota, the massive, nineteenth-century
apartment building where John Lennon had been
murdered. The intersection of Seventy-second

and Central Park West lay just a few hundred yards ahead, gridlocked by a couple of trucks stuck one behind the other.

"Oh, shit!" Zeus muttered.

McClane straightened out the wheel and kept his foot steady on the accelerator. There was the unmistakable sound of metal scraping metal as he rammed the car through the narrow space between the two trucks with barely an inch to spare. He rocketed through the entrance to Central Park, trailing a shower of sparks behind him.

The roadway just beyond the entrance curved down and to the right, a quick shortcut to Central Park South—if traffic was flowing. This morning, the line of cars started at the bottom of the hill and was stalled for as far as McClane could see.

"The park drive is *always* jammed!" Zeus was quick to tell him.

The guy was too uptight. McClane had a long history of extricating himself from impossible situations. All you had to do was be creative. A solution always presented itself.

The far left lane was permanently reserved for recreational use; no cars allowed. On the weekends, it was one big aerobics track. You crossed the road at your own risk. Even now, a weekday morning, it was packed with runners and walkers competing for space with high-speed bicyclists and rollerbladers.

He jerked the wheel to the left, dodged the

pack of bikers bearing down on him, and jumped the curb that separated the sidewalk from the road. A pair of long-limbed young women, dressed in tiny, brightly colored running shorts and halters, scooted out of the way, then shrieked their indignant protests at his invasion of their space. The taller one reminded him of Holly. Same coloring and hairstyle. Same eagerness to tell him he'd fucked up.

He glanced in the mirror. Walsh had attempted the same stunt, but the van hadn't made it over the curb. *So long, boys. See you downtown.*

"Didn't say the park drive. Said the park," he shouted at Zeus, who appeared to have gone into an advanced state of catatonia.

They were coming up on the Sheep Meadow, a grassy, fence-enclosed area with a spectacular view of the midtown skyline that was favored by sun worshippers, kite-flying enthusiasts, and families who preferred the more protected nature of the site. McClane veered right in a failed attempt to avoid crashing into the wire fence. They hit the fence sideways, ricocheted forward, and fishtailed across the grass.

He yanked the wheel, steering a hard right away from a bunch of high-school kids who looked like refugees from Woodstock, and maneuvered the cab between a couple of homeless men scavenging the garbage for recyclable cans and bottles. He didn't notice the boulder that jutted into the middle of the field until he was almost on top of it. The car tilted precariously on its side, but he made it over the top and landed squarely on all four wheels.

Zeus clutched the seat and prayed. From the moment he'd noticed McClane on the street, he'd suspected the guy was insane. Now he knew it for sure. He'd never seen anyone drive like this, not even in the movies. This crazy son-of-a-bitch cop thought he was another goddamned Evel Knievel!

Clutching the dashboard, he stared in horror as a young man grabbed for his Frisbee and barely missed catching a piece of the fender instead. Two lovers peacefully necking on a blanket made a quick escape by rolling down a hill, out of the path of the car. A mime in a clown's costume playacted an elaborate show of bravado as the car rocketed towards him, then bolted into the bushes just in the nick of time.

Zeus shook his head at the close call. "Are you aiming for these people?" he demanded.

"No," said McClane. He glanced in the rearview mirror and chuckled. "Well, maybe the mime."

He hoped Zeus wasn't losing his nerve, because the easy part was behind them. He still somehow had to get the car over the low stone wall that encircled the park and make it in one piece onto Central Park South. A car with wings would do it nicely—the Batmobile, or one of those James Bond 007 numbers that could fly on command.

But this was real life. Not a Batmobile in sight. Just a band of pigeons flapping their wings as they scattered and soared out of harm's way. One stayed behind and perched itself on another of the massive rocks that the park's designer had left in place when he'd created New York's biggest backyard. McClane stared at the pigeon; the pigeon stared back.

It was an invitation too good to resist. McClane aimed his front wheels as far up the rock as he could manage. The pigeon took off in a hurry. McClane followed him, using the rock as a launching pad to bounce over the wall and onto the hood of a car parked just on the other side.

They landed in the middle of traffic on Central Park South.

"How do Catholics do that thing?" Zeus said very quietly.

McClane smiled. "North, south, west, east."

With a shaky hand, Zeus made the sign of the cross.

"How much time?" asked McClane.

Zeus glanced at his watch. "Twenty-seven minutes."

"Seventy-second and Broadway to Central Park South in three minutes during rush hour?" McClane whooped triumphantly. Put *that* in the Ripley's book. Got to be a record."

Zeus felt sick to his stomach from their little joyride through the park. McClane's excitement seemed out of proportion, considering that they were once again stuck in traffic that had slowed almost to a standstill. "Yeah?" he said, pointing to the mess in front of them. "Now what?"

Cars and buses were moving at a dull, painful crawl. Even the bikers were having trouble threading their way through the dense wall of vehicles feeding into the streets that converged at Columbus Circle.

"We need a fire truck," he said sullenly.

McClane peered through the windshield. "I don't see a fire."

"To *follow,*" Zeus said.

That made twice today that Zeus's ingenuity had rescued them from a tight spot. The guy should have been a cop. "Gotcha," McClane said. He snapped his fingers. "Done deal."

He clicked on the cab's CB radio and impatiently fiddled with the dial until he found the police band.

"NYPD," said the switchboard operator. "May I help you?"

"Lieutenant John McClane, NYPD access ID number seven-four-seven-nine, calling from a civilian transmitter. Give me an emergency dispatcher."

He counted seconds. One, two . . . He heard

the phone ring, then another operator's voice
came over the band. "Nine-one-one."

It wasn't hard to summon up a sense of urgency, and the lie tripped off his tongue just as
easily. "Two officers down at the corner of Fourteenth Street and Ninth Avenue. Need an ambulance! Over!"

He tossed the radio mike to Zeus. "Emergency
calls on the west side go to Roosevelt Hospital.
That's two blocks from here."

They inched toward the intersection and advanced two car lengths before the light changed.
Now, they were stuck next to the stone fountain
momument to Christopher Columbus that
guarded the southwest entrance to the park. Mc-
Clane decided, the hell with it. He had an ambulance to chase, a train to catch at Wall Street. He
floored the gas and jumped the median. The cab
slammed into the base of the fountain, careened
across Broadway, and veered right, heading west
on Fifty-seventh Street toward Roosevelt.

His timing was impeccable. Its siren blaring,
an ambulance roared out of the hospital driveway
and turned right onto Ninth Avenue. McClane
gave himself a second to gloat as he pulled in
right behind it and headed south.

Zeus had to hand it to him. The ambulance
ploy was brilliant. If there was one thing New
Yorkers still paid attention to, it was the ear-split-
ting blast of the siren, warning them to get out of

the way. All along Ninth Avenue, cars pulled over to clear a path, and traffic on the side streets came to a dead halt. The ambulance ignored the red lights and zipped through one empty intersection after another, running interference for McClane and Zeus, who whizzed along in its wake.

The speedometer started at forty and quickly swung past fifty to sixty. When it surged toward seventy, Zeus stopped watching and kept his eyes glued to the road. This was better than the Indy 500!

"That's the ticket! Pick up some blockers and go for the end zone!" McClane shouted as they shot past Twenty-third Street.

"If you'd said Wall Street, we could have followed 'em all the way," Zeus shouted back.

McClane shook his head. "Wrong. Calls below Fourteenth Street go to a different hospital. St. Vincent's."

He glanced at Zeus and grinned. "You're good at math? I'm good at traffic."

At Fourteenth Street, the ambulance skidded to a stop, and the paramedics jumped out. They hastily fanned out along the busy shoplined street, madly searching for the wounded officers they'd been summoned to care for.

McClane veered right to avoid them, cleared the intersection, and turned left. The streets got weird down here. Ninth Avenue suddenly changed identities, turned into Hudson Street, a northbound thoroughfare. He flew across Fourteenth, pumping the gas pedal. "Time?" he demanded.

"Ten-oh-two. We're halfway there with eighteen minutes to go."

"We're hitting traffic again," said McClane. He scowled as he tried to picture an alternate route. The Wall Street Broadway line station was all the way east, almost at the river. No way they could make it in the time they had left, not even if they were following a whole fleet of ambulances. There were too many twists and turns, too many little streets that veered off in the wrong direction, especially the closer they got to Wall Street. He had only one option, a long shot, but it just might work.

"Fuck this," he said. It had to work. It was the only card in his hand he had left to play.

He braked so abruptly that Zeus was thrown forward against the dashboard.

"What now?" Zeus grumbled, grateful for the seat belt that had kept him from flying through the windshield.

McClane was already out the car. "We're probably ahead of that train. . . ."

Zeus suddenly realized McClane had pulled over next to the subway station at Fourteenth and Seventh Avenue. He knew what McClane was thinking, but he couldn't believe it. "You're not . . . !"

"I'm getting on it. You get to the phone by 10:20. I get to the bomb. You fail, I got you covered. I fail, you cover me."

"And if we both fail?"

"We're fucked." McClane sprinted towards the station. "Go!"

Zeus unhooked his belt, slid across to the driver's seat, and watched McClane disappear into the station. "My lucky fuckin' day," he muttered. He was back where he'd started, driving a cab. He checked his watch. Screw Simon and screw McClane. Now he had less than eighteen minutes to get all the way to Wall Street.

Chapter 5

McClane raced down the stairs. He reached the track level just in time to see the doors closing on the Number Three. "Shit!" he yelled, startling a pair of nuns who had just gotten off the train and come through the turnstile.

He bounded back up the steps and dashed south on Seventh Avenue for half a block until he found a ventilation grate. Maybe Holly was right, he thought, as he ripped open the grate. Maybe he was getting too old for this kind of work. He dropped down several meters into the tunnel and landed catlike, on all fours. He grinned in the darkness when he realized he was exactly where he wanted to be—on the roof of the train that had just left the station.

Or maybe not. If a cat had nine lives, he had to be good for at least a couple more.

He swung over the side, kicked in the window

of the conductor's compartment, and swung himself inside. He fell forward into the lap of the conductor. The startled man awoke screaming from a nap and gawked at him in terror.

McClane shook his head in disgust. Talk about being asleep at the wheel. He flipped his shield in the conductor's face and was rewarded with a yawn.

"Go back to sleep," he said. Then he hurried into the first car to start checking for suspicious-looking packages, for that "something provocative," as Simon had put it.

Provoke his ass, thought McClane. He was going to win this goddamn game—no matter what Simon said.

Tribeca. Short for "Triangle Below Canal." Zeus hadn't been this far downtown since he'd opened his shop. And that had to be . . . hell, a good six, seven years ago. Not much had changed. Abandoned warehouses sat side by side trendy new restaurants and expensively renovated lofts, homes to up-and-coming artists, filmmakers, and scene-makers. The twin towers of the World Trade Center loomed ahead, growing clearer against the bright blue summer sky the closer he got to the oldest part of the city.

He'd always hated driving a cab. Cabbies were sitting ducks for every punk and junkie with a knife or a gun who was looking to pick up some spare change. They couldn't hope to get a whole lot more than that. Even on his best days, he hadn't earned much more than a hundred dollars or so. His back used to hurt so bad from sitting hunched over the wheel for almost twelve hours straight that he'd have to go home and sleep on the floor, just to get some relief.

He'd been robbed only once, but he'd been cheated more times than he cared to remember by people who should have known better than to give a fifty-cent tip on an eight- or ten- or twelve-dollar fare. Not to mention all the times he'd picked up a man in a pin-stripped suit or a woman wrapped in furs at some fancy Park Avenue address, only to have them puke their guts out all over his backseat and allow him the privilege of cleaning up their mess.

Oh, yes, he'd seen it all. He could teach Detective John McClane a thing or two about the city, he thought, making the turn onto Broadway, which would take him over to Wall.

He coasted down past Reade Street, then suddenly had to slam on the brakes when he hit City Hall Park. A huge tractor-trailer truck, a sixteen-wheeler, straddled the intersection of Chambers and Broadway. He screeched to a halt, tapped his fingers, and waited for the monster to heave itself out of his way. Precious seconds were passing. Only six minutes left before Simon was due to call. He had to be there when the phone rang. He'd never forgive himself if he weren't.

It wasn't until he heard the man's voice that he realized someone had pulled open the door and was sliding into the backseat of the cab.

"One-twelve Wall Street," the man said.

Zeus spun around and stared at a white middle-aged man, exactly the type of arrogant, three-piece suit business honky he used to hate when he was driving. "Wait! This isn't a cab! You don't understand!" he protested.

The man fanned himself with his *Wall Street Journal.* "Your light's on," he said crisply. "I'll make it simple. One-twelve Wall Street or I'll have your medallion suspended." He snapped open the paper, then peered over the top. "Don't you like white people?" he sneered.

Zeus felt his blood pressure rising as his passenger leaned back and buried his nose in the newspaper. Yeah, sure the light was on, signaling that the cab was free for hire. But did his face match the photo ID on the dashboard? Not unless he'd somehow metamorphosed from a dark-skinned, handsome African-American into a pale, watery-eyed Russian named Vladimir. But there was no point wasting valuable seconds arguing with Mr. Three-Piece Suit.

"One-twelve Wall Street?" he said. "You got it."

   Hell, yes, he'd give him a ride to the office—a
ride he'd remember for the rest of his life.

The train hurtled through the tunnel, looping
eastward en route to Wall Street. McClane
counted the stops until his final destination—
Chambers Street, Park Place, Fulton Street—as
he made his way from car to car, searching for
Simon's bomb. By now, the train was only half-
filled; the majority of the commuters who worked
downtown in the courts, city government, or financial district had to be at work by nine-thirty,
at the latest, and it was already past ten o'clock.
   Most of the passengers were too absorbed in
their paperback novels and newspapers to notice
him hurrying down the aisle. A couple of lady
lawyers, identically dressed for success in somber
suits, pearls, and pumps, adjusted their skirts and
glared at him as he stooped to peer beneath their
seats.
   Sorry, babes, he thought, *but I'm busy.* They
weren't even his type. Too serious and severe.
Holly at least knew how to laugh. Or used to.
Maybe she'd turned into one of these grim-faced
women who believed all men were scum.
   Nah, he decided, winking at the women as he
moved on to the next car. Holly was too smart for
that. He knew how her mind worked. Only *he* was
scum. She'd decide about the rest of mankind on
a case-by-case basis.

* * *

The tip of Manhattan was narrow and dark and difficult to negotiate. Too many people in too small a space with not enough room between the streets for the sun to shine through among the tall buildings. Zeus avoided the area as much as possible. This was strictly white man's territory, where the lawyers and stockbrokers and bond traders spent their days figuring out how to keep all the wealth concentrated in their greedy little hands.

Like Mr. Three-Piece-Suit, whose angry comments about Zeus's driving had subsided into pathetic whimpers as Zeus had run yellow lights, mounted sidewalks, and zipped around corners at fifty and sixty miles an hour in order to get to the phone on time.

Zeus ignored him—left him hyperventilating and flattened against the back seat—when he finally got to Wall Street. He abandoned the cab on a curb and raced down the stairs of the station.

Shit. He didn't have a token. *Be there, Mc-Clane,* he prayed, then gracefully leapfrogged over the turnstile.

A young transit cop, munching on a doughnut as he kept watch over the sparse midmorning flow, shouted, "Hey!" and chased after him.

Zeus didn't even spare him a glance. The phone . . . where was the fucking phone? The digital clock that hung from the station's ceiling

read 10:18. *It's cool, stay calm,* he told himself.
He raced across the platform, thinking, two minutes, two mintues to go. Gotta find . . . the phone
. . . there it was! And right next to it was some
goddamn yuppie businessman, checking his
pockets for change.

Zeus darted a look at the clock—10:19. Where
the hell was that express train? Had it already
come through the station? Better question: where
the hell was McClane?

He'd almost reached the end of the train when he
checked his watch and saw it was 10:19. They
couldn't be more than a minute out of Wall
Street. The package had to be here, had to be hidden somewhere in one of these last couple of
cars. He was counting on Zeus to be at the phone
right now, waiting for it to ring. But Simon
wouldn't be satisfied unless both of them were
there to do his bidding. He had to find the bomb,
in case Simon reached Zeus before the train
pulled into the station.

The train was air-conditioned, but sweat was
pouring down his neck and back, and his shirt
was soaked through with perspiration. He jerked
open the rear door of the car and breathed in a
lungful of the stale, fetid air blowing past him in
the tunnel. The train lurched sideways as it
rounded a curve. A rat skittered by on the track.

He grabbed at the guardrail, shoved open the door, and stepped into the next car.

He got as far as the middle of the car when he finally spotted what he'd been looking for. Simon's little calling card was mounted on a hook on the wall, just above an advertisement for a doctor who specialized in repairing torn earlobes.

Oblivious to the stares of the other passengers, he stood up on the seat beneath the ad and examined the device. It was the same kind of bomb he'd seen in Cobb's office—two vials, one filled with clear liquid, the other with red. He gingerly peeled the contraption off the wall and carefully stepped down from the seat. He tried not to think about the fact that at this precise second, Simon might be sending the signal by remote control beeper that would detonate the bomb. Very slowly, he walked toward the back of the train, determined to dispose of the bomb before it disposed of him.

Zeus was getting bug-eyed from glancing between the digital clock and the yuppie who was hogging the phone while he dug for coins. The clock was just flipping to 10:20 when the yuppie finally found a quarter and slipped it into the pay phone slot.

"Uh, sir, I'm expecting a call," Zeus said in his most pleasant tone. "I need that phone."

"Drop dead," said the yuppie.

Zeus remembered how polite McClane had been to the woman at the Seventy-second Street booth. ''Please, sir,'' he said quietly. ''This is important.''

The yuppie didn't even bother looking at him. ''Listen, bro. I was here first.''

'' 'Bro'?'' He glared at the yuppie, another fucked-up white boy who'd watched too many Spike Lee movies. Screw being polite. Another thirty seconds of this shit, and they'd all be dead. ''Get away from the goddamn phone!'' he screamed.

The yuppie hastily replaced the receiver and backed away in alarm. At that same moment, another voice rang out with the words Zeus had hoped never to hear again in his life: ''Get your hands up!''

He froze. Slowly, very slowly, he turned his head in the direction of the voice. A transit cop stood no more than ten feet away, his gun aimed at Zeus's chest.

He raised his hands. The phone rang.

''Look, I have to answer that,'' he told the cop.

It rang again.

''Shut up and get your hands in the air!'' the cop yelled.

The phone rang a third time.

Suddenly, there was the unmistakeable sound of the train approaching the station.

The phone rang a fourth time.

A bullet in his chest or his butt blow sky-high. Life was all about making choices.

"I'm a cop!" McClane yelled. He could feel the device beginning to vibrate in his hands. The red liquid was starting to shoot into the clear. "Move! Get out! This is a bomb!"

This was New York. Anything was possible. The few remaining passengers scrambled away from him and rushed toward the front of the train.

The clear liquid was now stained a bright pink. Most of the red liquid had drained out of the vial. As tenderly as if he were holding a baby, McClane set the bomb down on the last seat of the last car. He pulled the handle of the rear door. Nothing happened. He jerked the handle again. It still wouldn't open. His watch read 10:20. Was this some kind of cosmic bad joke? Would the last laugh be Simon's?

Zeus was keeping count. Five rings. Six. How many more before Simon would hang up and set off the bomb? He couldn't take the risk.

He took a deep breath and began speaking in a quiet, measured tone, trying to reassure the cop that he didn't want trouble. "I must answer that phone," he said. "If you have to shoot me for that, then that's what you've gotta do. But I have to answer."

Leaving one hand in the air, he allowed the

other one to float out to one side and touch the phone. He kept his eyes on the cop as he gently removed the receiver from its cradle. "Yes, I'm here."

The cop took a step closer.

"Where is McClane?" asked Simon.

Good question. Zeus was wondering the same thing himself. What was the right answer? What would McClane say? "He's on his way. He doesn't move as fast as I do. He's out of shape."

Simon didn't even chuckle. "The rules were both of you," he reminded Zeus. "I'm afraid this is noncompliance. Good-bye."

The dial tone in Zeus's ear was drowned out by the much louder noise of the train roaring into the station. He could see the glare of the headlights emerging from the tunnel.

He dropped to the ground. "Trust me!" he yelled at the cop. "Duck!"

The door wouldn't budge. But the door had a window. McClane turned sideways, stepped back a couple of feet to get some leverage, and smashed his shoulder through the glass panel. He brushed away the jagged shards and picked up the bomb. Summoning every bit of strength he had left, he wound his arm like a pitcher and hurled the bomb as far out over the tracks as he could manage. Then he threw himself onto the floor and waited for whatever Simon had planned.

* * *

The first car had just entered the far end of the station when its front wheels hit a black metal disk so tiny that even the most alert driver would never have noticed it. The disk, an electronic sensor, flashed in the darkness beneath the train. Its deadly signal reached the bomb as it hung in mid-air over the track. Detonation was instantaneous.

Zeus heard the explosion—a deafening blast that reverberated through the station—and shifted into automatic pilot. He pulled the transit cop to safety and shoved the yuppie back against the wall. Then he covered his head and prayed for God's mercy. People screamed and scattered and dived for the exits, as the rear car, wrenched by the blast from the rest of the train, flew sideways and came crashing down onto the platform. It catapulted across the length of the station and struck the stairs with a clang that boomed loudly enough to be heard clear across the Hudson to New Jersey.

A cloud of acrid gray smoke filled the station. Water suddenly rained from the emergency sprinklers in the ceiling. The lights flickered out, and the station was plunged into total darkness. There were more screams of hysteria, the clatter of bricks falling like hail, the clamor of sirens at street level. Then the backup generator kicked in, providing a dim illumination that only added to the eeriness of the scene.

Zeus's eyes stung from the thickening billows of smoke, and he could smell the fire burning in the tunnel. He pulled himself to his feet and peered through the murk at the subway car lying sideways against the stairs. Damn Simon! And damn that asshole McClane, or whatever bits and pieces remained of him after the explosion, for being so reckless and self-destructive.

He blinked, rubbed his eyes, blinked again. Considering what he'd just been through, he felt in pretty good shape; shaken up, but no obvious serious injuries. But he must have taken a hit to the head, because he was definitely seeing things. Not double vision, which he would have expected, but a much more traumatic illusion: McClane, bloodied and streaked with soot, woozily climbing out the subway window.

A crater-shaped pit had appeared in the middle of the park above the station. The streets were snarled with emergency personnel vehicles. While firemen sprayed the area with a chemical retardant to prevent the fire in the tunnel from spreading above ground, emergency medical service technicians were treating the wounded and loading the more serious cases onto ambulance stretchers. Uniformed cops had quickly thrown up wooden barricades to keep out the inevitable crowd of rubberneckers who wanted to get as close as possible to the scene. Reporters from all the media were shouting questions at the police and trying to interview anyone who emerged from the station.

The second explosion of the morning—and this one at Wall Street, America's financial center—was *big* news, a major story. The reporters all wanted confirmation that the two bombings were linked. Cobb had promised to fire anyone who so much as nodded at the press. Not a word from anyone. Period, the end.

The veteran reporters recognized McClane when he and Zeus staggered up the steps. They were all over him for a statement, but he brushed past them to join his colleagues for an update. An EMS team quickly checked him for broken bones, then washed and bandaged his cuts. He ignored their urging that he take a ride to the nearest hospital, to get X-rayed for internal bleeding, and collared Lambert for a report on the injuries.

"A couple concussions, an old guy's pacemaker stopped, and a pregnant girl's water broke. That's it. You pulled off a miracle, Johnny," Lambert said admiringly.

McClane frowned. "That's the problem. The miracle part. Ever feel like a game was rigged for you to lose?"

Zeus shook his head. "You had to get to forty for this? White boys."

"I'm serious," said McClane. "What're the chances we'd make it down here? Zip, right?

That bomb was going off. He *wanted* it to go off—right here.''

"In the subway?'' Lambert asked.

McClane stared at the crater, the sound of the explosion still ringing in his ears. "Something doesn't add up.''

"Lieutenant McClane?'' A uniformed cop called to him. "Inspector Cobb wants to see you.'' He pointed to a van parked in an alley to the right of the station. "The van, down there.''

SAMSON'S MOVERS said the logo on the side of the van. McClane eyed the two men dressed in overalls and sunglasses who stood in front of the van, conferring with Cobb. If those two were movers, then his name was Marilyn Monroe. When were the Feds ever going to learn that they had to give up the standard-issue fifties Brylcreem look if they wanted to go undercover?

He gestured to Zeus to come with him, and went to join his boss. Cobb ushered them inside the van, where two more Brylcreem men in conservatively-cut suits were waiting for them.

"John, this is Andy Cross of the FBI,'' said Cobb. "And this is Bill Jarvis. He's—''

"With another agency,'' Jarvis cut him off. "Good to meet you.''

"Lieutenant McClane and Mr. Carver,'' said Cobb, completing the introductions.

As they exchanged handshakes, McClane noticed a third, somewhat older man standing at the

back of the van. Like the men outside, he was
wearing dark glasses and flipping through a magazine, though McClane noticed his head was
cocked in their direction and he was turning the
pages too quickly to be reading them.

"We've got just a couple of questions," Cobb
said, smiling as if they were all old friends.

He showed McClane a color photograph of a
hollow-cheeked man with thinning black hair
standing next to a beautiful young woman.

"Have you ever seen this man?" he asked.

McClane shook his head.

"Or this one?"

The second picture appeared to have been
taken in a café or restaurant, probably with the
kind of long-distance, telephoto lens favored by
covert operation types. The subject was a middle-
aged, dark-haired man, possibly European, with
aristocratic features. The man was smiling, probably at someone whose face had been cropped
out of the picture. But the smile was taut, the
lines around his mouth emphasizing the severity
of his demeanor, and his blue eyes were hard and
icy cold.

"How about you?" Cross asked Zeus, who
gave him the same negative response as Mc-
Clane.

"Did you recognize the voice?" Cross asked
McClane.

Like he wouldn't have mentioned it before if

he had. These guys were a waste of taxpayers' money. "Yeah, it was definitely Buffalo Bob. Come on," he said disgustedly.

Cross and Jarvis exchanged glances, then Jarvis took over the questioning. "Have you had any sense you were being followed lately, or that you were under surveillance?"

"Well, there's this chick who . . ." McClane began. The two men eagerly leaned forward, and he realized they thought he was serious. He said, "Cut it the fuck out! Who are these guys? What do you people know?"

There was another long, meaningful glance between the two agents.

Then Jarvis said, "We've read your jacket, Lieutenant. And we were told you'd be cooperative."

Cobb spoke up before McClane had a chance to shoot off his mouth. "He will be. But if you want us to share information, you might try sending a little the other way."

"We'd like to hear what he knows first," Cross said.

McClane threw up his hands. "Okay! Hold it!"

Cross smiled again, as if he'd known all along that McClane would come through for them.

"We've got a mad bomber," said McClane. "He calls himself Simon. He speaks German. Knows a shitload about bombs. Doesn't give a damn about money. And for some reason, he's really pissed at me! Happy?''

They looked anything but happy—even Cross had stopped smiling. But he'd made his point. Jarvis shot his eyes over to the man in the back, who nodded almost imperceptibly.

Permission granted.

''The first man is Mathais Targo. Was Hungarian military. Explosives expert. We believe he works for the Iranians now,'' Jarvis said.

''Works?'' Cobb asked.

''Freelance terrorism. By contract.''

McClane pointed to the woman next to Targo. ''Who's the girl?''

''Targo's other half. All we know is her first name's Katya,'' Cross said. ''Rumor is the Israelis tried to slip a bomb between their sheets. He wasn't home. They think maybe they got her.''

''The second man was an obscure colonel in the East German Army,'' Jarvis continued. ''Ran an infiltration unit. Sort of thing the Nazis tried in the Battle of the Bulge. English-speaking troops behind our lines. About all we know of him is GDR medical records indicating he suffers from migraines. His name is Peter Krieg.''

''Boy, I gotta hand it to you! You nailed 'em! You got Boris, Natasha, and the baby colonel makes three. Somebody wanna explain what the hell this has got to do with me?'' McClane demanded.

The information well suddenly went dry.
All those words, and something was missing.
Some important piece of data they were holding
back . . .

He motioned toward the man in the back. "The
answer on his face?"

The older man put down his magazine. "The
name Gruber mean anything to you, Lieutenant?" he asked.

McClane stiffened. Gruber. That bastard. He
would never forget Hans Gruber—nor the image
of his body falling hundreds of feet from the top
of the Nakatomi Towers.

"Rings a bell," he admitted. "Why?"

Cobb poked Walsh. Who the hell was Hans
Gruber?

"That thing in the building in LA," whispered
Walsh.

"Peter Krieg was born Simon Peter Gruber.
He's Hans Gruber's brother," said the man in the
back.

They were joking. Had to be. That was history.
Did they really believe that Simon had stolen all
those tons of explosives and was coming after
him because of what had happened to his
brother?

"So yeah," Cross said, nodding, "this is about
that thing in LA. We figure he's got McClane fitted for a toe tag. And he's gonna do just about
anything to see it tied on."

McClane was about to tell him they must have it figured all wrong when Cobb's secretary leaned into the van and handed her boss a cellular phone. "Inspector, it's him," she said.

"You didn't tell him who we're with, did you?" asked Cobb.

"Of course not," she said, insulted that he even had to ask.

Cross reached for the phone. "Here." He set it into a cradle that was wired to a speaker, pushed a button, and signaled that the microphone in front of them was active.

"Simon?" said Cobb.

The terrorist's voice filled the space. "Inspector. Who from the FBI is there? Let's see . . . probably Cross. Say hello, Andrew."

Cross looked helplessly at the man at the back, who sighed softly and shrugged.

"Hello," Cross said.

Simon chuckled. "I know you never run alone. Say hello, Bill. You still trying to look really butch by chewing on your sunglasses?"

Jarvis snatched his glasses out of his mouth and scowled.

Simon laughed again, then quickly cut himself off. "This, as they say, is where the plot thickens," he said, no longer sounding amused. "I have put twenty-four hundred pounds of explosives in one of the fourteen hundred forty-six schools in greater New York. It is fitted with a timer set to explode at exactly three P.M.''

Nobody said a word. The idea was simply too shocking. The potential for a hideous tragedy was horrifying. The worst part was that not one of them doubted Simon was telling the truth.

''Thank you. Your silence says I am understood,'' said Simon.

''Did you say twenty-four hundred pounds?'' Cobb stammered.

''Yes. Don't interrupt again.''

Cobb flushed deep red as the terrorist continued, ''Simon says, if you attempt to evacuate schools, the bomb will be detonated by radio—and gentlemen, someone will be watching. Repeat. One school will be permanently dismissed at three P.M. Unless . . .''

His voice trailed off.

Determined not to lose more face in front of the feds, Cobb forced himself to ask the question. ''Unless what?''

''Unless John McClane and his new best friend complete the tasks I set them. John, are you listening?''

McClane's eyes were closed. He was thinking about the taste of scotch over ice cubes. But he was listening. ''Yeah,'' he said. What the hell else would he be doing?

''The pay phone beyond hope. Tompkins Square Park, twenty minutes. Go by foot. No rush. Give yourself time to think. To enjoy the power of life and death I've bestowed on you. Oh, by the way, gentlemen, we got something of a bargain on radio detonators. The only problem is the damned things seem to respond to police and FBI frequencies. So I'd avoid using your radios.''

"Simon, wait!" Cobb said.

He was gone as abruptly as usual.

There was another moment of silence, as the implications of Simon's latest threat sank in.

"Twenty-four hundred pounds of that liquid stuff? My God!" Cobb exclaimed. "Get hold of the commissioner," he told his secretary.

"Doing a press conference, supposed to be here in half an hour," she reminded him.

Cobb swallowed hard, tasting the acid accumulating in his stomach. "All right." He turned to Walsh and said, "Ricky, get every senior officer on site. Gather them here. Now."

Walsh was already out the door as Cobb turned to Cross. "You going to give us some sort of jurisdictional nonsense?"

"I got two kids in school on Sixty-fourth Street," Cross bleakly replied. "How can we help you?"

"How many men you got?"

"Seventy-five in the city. We hit the panic button, we can get five hundred on the way from Washington."

"When?"

"Two-thirty, three," Cross said apologetically.

Too late, but who knew what other surprises Simon had in store? Couldn't hurt to have more FBI around in case they were needed. "Get them moving. But we're gonna have to do this ourselves," he told Cross. He nodded at McClane and Zeus. "Tompkins Square Park is more than two miles. You two better start running. No radios. Take my phone. When you get something, call me through the switchboard. Good luck."

McClane stuck the phone in his pocket. "Thanks," he said, meaning it.

Tompkins Square was in the East Village, a good forty-five minute walk on a nice, cool day. Simon had given them twenty minutes, and the mercury had to be hitting ninety. Hans Gruber's brother was a fucking sadist, which didn't surprise him. It ran in the family.

They took off briskly from the van. Half a block later, McClane was already wondering whether he could make it to the East Village without falling flat on his face. It was too damn hot to be walking, let alone jogging. Hoping some conversation might help to distract him, he said, "Truthfully, Zeus. How hateful am I?"

Zeus smirked. "No comment."

"I mean, a guy's doing life for attempted murder of a whole fucking government. So he blows his way out and risks it all just to do me?'' he said, gasping for breath.

''What's the matter, McClane?'' Zeus eye-balled the cop. ''You got low self-esteem?''

He shook his head as they trotted in place, waiting for the light to change at Maiden Lane. ''I don't know,'' he said, utterly frustrated. ''Goddamn it, I don't know.''

Cobb watched the two men jog up Pearl Street. They were gone from sight by the time Walsh returned to the van with the senior officers present.

''Senior is Chief Allen,'' he informed Cobb, gesturing to the white-haired man on his right.

''Of what?''

''Transit.''

Cobb nodded at him and the other men in command of the various groups working together to clean up after the bomb. ''Gentlemen, we have to make a decision,'' he announced, fully aware that it would probably be the most important one of his career. ''And because of time, we'll have to bring our bosses aboard later. The man who did this says he's put a very large bomb in one of the schools in the New York area. And he says we can't evacuate. But he didn't say we can't search.''

He stopped to make sure they were following him. These were all men like himself, people who'd spent their adult lives trying to protect

their fellow New Yorkers. They understood what
it meant to implement this type of labor-inten-
sive, large-scale action without the proper autho-
rization. His job was on the line, but too many
lives were at stake—too many *children's*
lives—to hesitate.

Hoping he had their support, he said, ''I rec-
ommend we get everybody—and I mean *everybody*—police, fire, sanitation, the transit, even the
goddamn librarians, and we start searching
schools! Right now! That's maybe a thousand
buildings in the city limits and three hours, forty-
five minutes to do it in. He said the bomb is tuned
to our radios, so we use telephones, rip the radios
right out of their hands if you have to. And we've
got to try to keep the media out of it as long as
possible, or we'll have a panic. Have I your agreement?''

''Make it happen. We'll clean up the damn politics later,'' Allen said without hesitation, and the
other men nodded their agreement. ''Let's go,
gentlemen,'' he said. ''We've got a lot to do.''

The officers left the van to organize their
forces. Cobb turned to Walsh and said, ''Ricky,
you hold down the fort here while we try to get
this organized. Take everybody in this whole
goddman horde—Joe, Connie, Phil, everyone—
and push 'em north to start leapfrogging schools.
We'll clean up the niceties later. Let's move!''

Chapter 6

From the top of a roof ten floors above Wall Street, Simon Gruber and Mathias Targo had an unobstructed view of the station. The people on the ground below them looked like tiny plastic windup toys scurrying in every direction.

"They bought it," Simon Gruber said with an ironic smile. "You can begin."

Targo, his colleague in terror, watched the police cars fly away from the crime scene like chickens fleeing from the butcher's knife. He switched on his radio and quietly spoke a few words in German.

Less than a mile away, at an abandoned pier that jutted into the East River, a fleet of dump trucks was parked with engines at idle. The men seated in the trucks had been handpicked by Simon and Targo. They'd spent months in the desert training for this mission, and its success depended in part on their split-second timing. Now, at Targo's signal, they shifted their gears into first and began filing out of the pier, headed for Wall Street.

Simon's thin lips creased again in a smile. "Hook, line, and sinker," he said.

He was very pleased. His plan was proceeding precisely as he'd anticipated.

Assured by Walsh and the others that there was no story to cover, the newspaper and radio reporters had already drifted out of the park. But the TV news teams were more persistent, less easily persuaded that two explosions in one morning was just a crazy coincidence. Competition for ratings was tough in the local market, and big stories meant big ratings. Explosions, especially in the subway, made New Yorkers very, very nervous. They wanted to know who, what, and why—and they wanted to know it *now.* The TV correspondents had orders not to leave without a statement that would translate into a sexy sound bite.

Walsh sympathized, but he, too, had his orders. "Nothing more to see, people. You gotta evacuate," he insisted, trying to shoo the reporters away from the park.

They were all talking at once, calling out questions. "No leads? No demands? Have you called in the FBI? Are you saying this isn't linked to the Bonwit's bomb?"

"All I'm saying, we got things under pretty fair control, and you gotta clear the area," he said.

Nobody moved. He crossed his arms against his chest and shook his head. No comment. They weren't going to get anything else out of him—or out of anyone else connected with the investigation.

Every city worker in a uniform who was present at the scene had gathered out of earshot of the reporters to hear Cobb's orders.

He briefly clued them in and told them about Simon's latest bomb threat. "I repeat," he said, staring at the sea of white and yellow and brown and black faces assembled in front of him. "All personnel. That means transit cops, Port Authority cops, airport cops, the fire department . . . everyone. We're gonna search every school, top to bottom. Quietly, plainclothes, out of uniform. 'Cause if the press or anyone find out, God help us. The panic would make the Blackout of 'Seventy-six look like a picnic."

They nodded their agreement. Many of them knew from first-hand experience what could happen when civilians panicked in a crisis. It only made their jobs harder—and this assignment was one of toughest they'd ever faced, especially for those who had kids in the school system.

Their commanding officers had already briefed

them on their assignments. They were eager to get moving. Cobb watched them disperse into their units. "Goddamn this guy," he muttered. The clock had already started ticking.

The calls went out to patrol supervisors all over the city: the NYPD captains in charge of security at Kennedy and LaGuardia Airports; their counterpart at the Triboro Bridge and Tunnel Authority; the heads of security at the Board of Education and the Sanitation Department; the Transit Authority captains in each of the city's five boroughs.

As each patrol car exited the garages, cops stationed at the doors collected the police band radios.

They all had their orders. Get out to the schools. Keep cool. Investigate every possibility. Check out anything that looked even slightly suspicious. Stay away from the police band. Any questions, dial 911.

Nobody had thought to warn Wanda Shepherd, the day shift supervisor at emergency police dispatch, the main switching center for police communication. Suddenly, the phones were ringing all at once at all twenty stations, as her 911 operators struggled to keep up with the huge increase in calls.

John Turley sighed when he saw her steaming

down the hall to his office, her usual cigarette hanging out of her mouth. The department's chief of internal communications, he was Wanda's boss, though he often wondered which of them actually gave the orders.

Her wiry gray hair stuck out in every direction as she charged through his doorway to demand an explanation.

"Sergeant Turley, the volume here has quadrupled in the last five minutes. What the hell is—"

"Stop," Turley calmly interrupted her. "Let me explain. For the rest of the day, we're handling all the department's communication."

Normally frenetic, this morning she was teetering on the edge of hysteria. "What do you mean 'all'?"

"We're shutting down the police band. All calls will be handled through this switchboard."

Wand finished her cigarette and immediately lit another. "And I'm gonna marry Donald Trump!" she yelled. "Do you have any idea what kind of volume we're talking?"

The department functioned as well as it did because Wanda ran a smooth, efficient operation in spite of her nervous nature. Today would be the ultimate test of her skills. She'd need all the help she could get.

Turley put his arm around her and walked her back to the dispatch room. "We'll deal with this as best we can," he said. "You want a Valium?"

*   *   *

The cops and firemen were all gone by the time
Simon and Targo came down from their observa-
tion post and strolled across the street to their
next destination. Targo silently noted the two cars
driving slowly toward the bomb site, then went
back to the argument he'd been having with
Simon since they'd left the building.

"Your game with this policeman is dangerous
and undisciplined," he said. "He got to the
bomb. Detonation was three hundred feet short of
target."

Simon's game, as Targo choose to call it, had
been carefully conceived and implemented. He
would no more abandon his pursuit of McClane
than he would abort the rest of the mission. "Is
the subway not closed? Did the roof not collapse?
The rest is inconvenience, no more," he said dis-
missively.

Targo remained unconvinced. "And if it's too
far from the alarms?"

"If we have a problem, we will deal with it."

Targo shook his head. "We shouldn't have to.
I should factor him out now."

"Patience," counselled Simon. "He keeps the
police busy. Keeps their noses pointed where we
want them pointed. Gives them a sense of accom-
plishment. Let them stand still and one of them is
liable to start thinking. We'll run McClane
around for another hour or so, and then collect

him.'' He glanced sideways at his partner as he
bent down to tie his shoe. ''If you must worry
like an old woman, then worry whether the package was successfully delivered to that particular
school.''

Out of the corner of his eye, he saw that the
passengers from the two cars were walking parallel with himself and Targo toward the subway.
They were dressed for work: one group in business suits and ties, the other in flannel shirts and
jeans, a typical crew of construction workers.

Excellent. Thus far, they were right on
schedule.

There was one in every crowd, the guy who just
wouldn't quit. Walsh flinched as Ben Dunham
sauntered over, followed by his camera crew.
Dunham was the rising star of the number one
TV news team, with both the good looks and relentless curiosity it took to succeed as an investi-
gative reporter. Everyone else had given up on
the story and left. But not Dunham. He was still
nosing around, hunting for clues, asking questions that Walsh wasn't supposed to answer.

''Hey, Walsh! What's going on? Why'd everybody tear out of here?'' he said, coming up and
offering him a stick of gum.

Walsh shook his head to the gum and said,
''Look at your watch, coming up on shift change.
Once the bean counters found out nobody got

killed, they started screaming about no overtime. Had to get everybody back to precinct to punch out. The new shift will be pulling in in a few minutes.''

His response was so clever he impressed even himself. But Dunham wasn't buying it. "You're so full of shit, Walsh," he said, shoving the gum in his mouth.

Before Walsh could dispute Dunham's comment, he was distracted by a loud rumbling sound. "What the hell?" he said.

Fearing a tunnel collapse, he ran across the square to investigate. He didn't get very far before a man grabbed his arm, flashed his ID card, and introduced himself. "Bob Thompson, city engineer's office. We're gonna try to get an idea of the damage." The man looked down into the crater and whistled. "Holy Toledo! Somebody had fun!"

The rumbling sound grew more intense. A parade of dump trucks was coming around the corner, pulling into the square.

"Boy, you got here quick enough," he told the engineer, who was accompanied by seven or eight associates.

"Wall Street, son," Simon said heartily, in his best American accent. "Money. Lot of opinionmakers the mayor doesn't want to piss off. Appreciate it if you'd show my associates the way down."

"Sure thing." Walsh turned to one of the rookies who'd been assigned to help him patrol the site. "Jimmy, come on, you got the flashlight."

As Walsh nodded to Simon's people to follow him and Jimmy down into the subway station, Simon smiled his thanks and headed for his next appointment.

Targo and his crew fell in step behind Walsh. He led them to the one entrance that hadn't been sealed off and cautioned them to watch out for fallen debris. Captured in the high beam of Jimmy's flashlight, the subway platform looked like the setting for a grade-B horror movie. Smoke from the explosion still hung in the air.

They'd gotten as far as the token booth, moving towards the damaged car which lay twisted across the steps at the far end of the platform, when Walsh noticed that Bob Thompson's men were all wearing paratrooper boots with their business suits. One or the other, he could see, but together, the combination was odd enough to make him curious.

Cobb always said, "A good detective asks lots of questions." He opened his mouth to ask a couple of questions. Two men suddenly stepped forward and stuck Jimmy with what he recognized to be pressurized innoculators, high-tech stun guns that sent the rookie collapsing onto the floor. He grabbed for his gun. . . .

Targo's right-hand man, Otto, had been itching

to kill a cop. He smiled into the gloom as his bullet pierced Walsh's chest. He knew immediately that the shot was lethal.

Targo didn't give the dead man a second glance as he moved on to inspect the tunnel. Otto had done his job. The Bulgarian thug's efficiency in just such situations was the reason Targo kept him around and paid him handsomely.

Otto toed the body aside, then smiled again as he noticed the man's gold shield. He bent down, removed the shield, and stuck it in the breast pocket of his suit: the spoils of war.

From his vantage point across from the square, Simon allowed himself one quick, satisfied glance. The months of planning were about to pay off. The park above the subway station was filling up with equipment: a flatbed with a tank-mounted bridge and a mining machine pulled in, followed by a second flatbed jammed with skid-steer loaders, the mini-tractors used in warehouses to move heavy objects. Men dressed in police uniforms were spilling out of the backs of the dump trucks and hurrying to their positions. One team had already begun offloading the bridge and unfolding it into the mouth of the crater.

Simon glanced at his watch, straightened his tie, and nodded at Freddie, Nigel, and Ian, the three men he'd handpicked for this next piece of the operation. As they strolled up the block to the ornate, neo-Renaissance limestone building that housed the Federal Reserve Bank, they looked the very image of three prosperous European gentlemen, on their way to do business with one of the world's premier banking institutions.

An alarm shrilled in their ears as they came into the high-ceilinged lobby. Simon hadn't ever been inside the building before, but its layout and design were completely familiar. He'd spent so many hours poring over its architectural plans, that he could have walked its rooms in the dark without stumbling. Just as he knew there would be, two guards were seated at the reception desk. Two more stood behind them on either side of a metal detector.

Affecting a Dutch accent, he presented himself to the guards at the desk. "Please inform"—he consulted his card—"Mr. Little that Mr. Vanderfloog is here."

The guard picked up the phone and dialed a three-digit extension. Shouting to be heard above the noise of the alarm, he conveyed Simon's message. He nodded, then informed Simon that Mr. Little was on his way down.

One of Simon's men mouthed the word "alarm?" and raised a questioning eyebrow at him. Simon replied with the briefest shakest of his head. No need to worry. This, too, had been anticipated.

The ringing stopped suddenly, just as an elevator door opened onto the lobby, and a short, balding man bustled up to them.

"Mr. Vanderflug?" he said, unintentionally mispronouncing Simon's alias. "Felix Little, corporate relations. Sorry to keep you waiting. There was apparently an explosion in the subway, and it played hell with our alarms, I'm afraid."

Simon affected an air of concern. "I trust nothing's wrong?"

"Oh, good Lord, no. Safe and secure," Little assured him. "You were concerned about a currency exchange? We're not a commercial bank in the normal sense. We're primarily governments, central banks, that sort of thing. Aside from the Depository, of course."

"Of course." Simon nodded.

"And you're in the flower business, Mr. Vanderflug?"

"*Floog,*" said Simon, correcting the mispronunciation.

Little looked at him, puzzled. "Pardon?"

"*Floog,*" Simon repeated himself, emphasizing the final syllable. "Vander*floog.* I sell tulips."

"Oh! Yes, of course. Please, forgive me," Little said obsequiously.

He led Simon through the metal detector, as Simon's three colleagues used their pressurized innoculators to take out the guards at the desk.

Oblivious to the breach in his bank's security,

Little asked, "And your sales volume, Mr. Vanderfloog, would be?"

"Approximately three hundred million."

"Guiders per annum, I see."

"Dollars per month," Simon corrected him.

"Oh, I see! That would be three-point-six billion . . ." Little quickly did the calculation in his head. "Yes, goodness! That's quite significant, yes!" he exclaimed, clearly pleased by the possibility of handling such a significant account.

"Oh, no," he interrupted himself as Simon made a right turn. "Not that way, goodness, that's the vault elevator." He lowered his voice and whispered confidentially, "You see, our alarms are sonic and seismic, two things which, I'm afraid, don't react very well to explosions. In fact, this subway business dropped the whole thing in a cocked hat! Had to give up and pull the breakers on the whole thing! The repair people are down there now!"

"Good Lord!" Once again, Simon looked properly worried.

"Heavens-to-Betsy, if anyone knew!" Little clucked.

Behind them, felled by the terrorists' innoculators, the guards standing at the metal detector suddenly crumpled to the floor. One of their guns clattered against the marble floor. Little glanced around to find the source of the noise, then whirled back and gaped at Simon.

"But, but . . . I thought this was a currency
exchange?" he stammered, as Freddie and Ian
dragged the guards' bodies past him.

Simon chuckled. "Oh, I think we'll go straight
to the withdrawal," he said.

One shot of the innoculator, and Little was out
of commission as well. Nigel quickly stripped off
his business suit, beneath which he was wearing
a US Marshal's uniform. Then he hauled Little
out of sight, as Simon turned down the corridor
toward the vault.

Targo's men, meanwhile, had unfolded the bridge
to its fullest extension into the crater and driven
the mining machine down along the length of the
bridge onto the subway tracks. The machine operator maneuvered the machine into position and
aimed the powerful jaw-like shovel at the exploded subway car, bashing and compressing the
steel until it no longer blocked the tunnel. The
machine next broke through a guard railing and
into the tunnel itself.

Targo has brought into the tunnel a specially
marked map, which he and his chief engineer
consulted now as the mining machine moved into
place. They took measurements, checked their
notes, measured again, until they were satisfied
they'd found the exact spot on the tunnel wall
they'd been searching for.

Targo sprayed guide marks on the wall and signaled the machine operator to begin. The jaws attacked the concrete, chewing it into pebble-sized fragments, digging deeper and deeper past the tunnel surface.

He blew a whistle, signaling the men up top to begin sending the skidsteers down along the bridge. The dump trucks were lined up to follow them. The noise was deafening. Sparks were flying everywhere. The dank tunnel air was so thick with dust that it was difficult to draw a deep breath. It hardly mattered. A few more seconds, and they would break through the last layer of concrete.

He closed his eyes a moment and pictured the prize that lay on the other side: gold bars, mountains of them worth millions of dollars, stacked floor-to-ceiling in wire cubicles inside the vault of the Federal Reserve.

The marshal whose job it was to watch the video monitor outside the gold vault sat up in his chair and stared at the screen. Either he was imagining things, or the cubicles were rattling. He took a closer look and thought, *Earthquake? Here in New York City?* He shook his head, nah, couldn't be. But the cubicles were definitely shaking, and roaring sounds, as if from some kind of machinery, seemed to be coming from the other side of the wall.

He picked up the phone and called his backup

team. "You'd better get over here, something's going on," he began, watching the screen as what appeared to be a monstrous pair of automated jaws suddenly broke through the wall of the vault. *"Holy Shit!"* he screamed, and ran for the vault.

The marshal at the other end of the phone yelled, "C'mon!"

He and his partners charged down the hall. They were stopped short by Simon and his crew, which now included twelve men armed with machine guns.

"This isn't lethal," said Nigel as he quickly stepped forward and zapped them with his innoculator.

Simon rushed his men past the sleeping marshals toward the vault. They were halted by a sudden burst of gunfire. "Stay back!" shouted the marshal stationed outside the vault, pointing his pistol at them as he fumbled madly to unlock the rifle rack.

Simon glanced at the video monitor. The mining machine had broken through to the vault. Targo was the first to step through the gaping hole in the wall. He made straight for the vault's massive steel door and began cranking open the finely balanced mechanism.

The marshal had managed to rip loose a shot gun from the rack. He trained it on them, grabbed the phone, and punched the numbers for the front desk. "Call the police and get down here! I'm under attack!" he screamed.

There was a long silence. Behind him, the door slowly slid open and Targo glided out of the vault.

Finally, a voice the marshal didn't recognize responded to his cry for help. "Just relax, mate, and maybe you'll live through this."

The terror-stricken marshal dropped the phone and gawked at Simon and his men. Panicking, he pulled the trigger. A spray of bullets hit the corridor, as Targo crept up behind him and sliced a knife through his back. He pitched forward, instantly dead. They were home free.

Simon and Targo, followed by Nigel, hurried into the vault, where the skidsteers were flooding through the hole. "Bloody Fort Knox!" whooped Nigel, catching his first glimpse of the gold.

Simon gave the thumbs up signal, and the skidsteer drivers went to work, ripping off the doors to the cubicles, ramming bucket-first into the stacks, loading gold like gravel.

"The only thing man has never wasted nor destroyed," Simon murmured, as the first of the gold-laden skidsteers roared back into the tunnel to spill their precious cargo into the dump trucks. "Made into one thing, then another, throughout time. In my hand could be Antony's gift to Cleopatra. Charlemagne's crown. Michelangelo's payment for the Sistine Chapel. The House of Rothschild's first profit.''

In assembly-line fashion, the dump trucks crawled up the bridge, to be replaced by empty ones. The skidsteers turned around and crawled back into the vault to collect the next load.

Simon laughed out loud and grabbed a bar from a passing skidsteer. ''What Napoleon took from Prussia in 1912, what Bismarck took back, what America and Japan have taken from everyone since!'' he crowed. ''Every trading country in the world stores in this room! One hundred forty billion dollars! Ten times what's in Kentucky! Fort Knox is for tourists!''

When they crossed Delancy Street and angled east toward First Avenue, McClane started mentally counting the number of blocks they still had to cover before they got to the park. His body was drenched in sweat, his chest was tighter than a drum. Counting streets kept him from wondering whether he was going to have a heart attack and die right here on the Lower East Side. Every fruit stand and bodega they passed called to him, but he didn't dare stop to satisfy his thirst. On their schedule, at the pace they were going, every second mattered.

Zeus loped alongside him, his arms and legs pumping gracefully. ''What 'thing' in LA were they talking about? You famous or something?'' he suddenly asked.

''Yeah,'' McClane grunted. ''For about five minutes.''

''Let me guess. Rodney King.''

The pain in his chest was getting worse. ''Fuck you,'' he gasped. ''Nakatomi Tower. I threw Simon's little brother out a window. Guess he's pissed off about it.''

A grizzled homeless man shuffled by, shaking his head at the folly of their midday run.

''You mean I'm in this shit 'cause some white cop killed some other white asshole's kid brother?'' Zeus demanded.

''Which part of that am I supposed to feel worse about? The white part or the cop part?''

''Both.''

''Hey! I grew up eating macaroni and cheese, same as you,'' McClane rasped.

Zeus zipped ahead of him, angrily shouting, ''Well, you ain't the same as me, so shut up!''

Shit. Who'd started this conversation anyway?

They ran the remaining distance in silence. At Seventh Street, with the park entrance in sight, McClane summoned his last reserves of energy and caught up with Zeus. Half-dead from the herculean effort, he could hear the pay phone ringing as he stumbled into the park.

''Yes! McClane!'' he gasped, ripping the receiver off the hook.

"John, you're out of shape. It's embarrassing. You barely made it," Simon taunted him.

"We *all* barely make it, Simon," he said, still panting to catch his breath. "Now, what the hell do you want us to do?"

"What has four legs and is always ready to travel?" asked Simon. The question was punctuated with the sharp click of his hanging up.

Damn it! Not another riddle! Help! He glanced blankly at Zeus, who almost laughed out loud with relief. It was his nephew Raymond's favorite riddle . . . and the answer was right in front of their noses: the bronze statue of an elephant with water streaming out of its trunk that stood in the fountain a few yards away.

A briefcase similar to the one that had been discovered in Chinatown lay under the fountain. McClane snapped it open. Inside was a small scale attached to the same type of binary-liquid bomb he'd found in the subway, as well as a digital timer that read "5:00." Nestled next to the bomb was a cellular phone and a LED readout that said, HI! I'M A BOMB. YOU'VE JUST ARMED ME.

When the phone rang, McClane and Zeus almost butted heads grabbing for it. McClane was quicker on the draw.

"I trust you've gotten the message?" asked Simon.

McClane stared at the bomb. "Yeah, I got it. How do we shut it off?"

"Patience, John. The fountain. There should be two jugs."

They easily located the two plastic jugs. McClane didn't even want to think about what could have happened if some kid or bum had found them before he did.

"A five-gallon jug and a three-gallon jug," said Simon. "Fill one of the jugs with exactly four gallons of water, and place it on the scale. The timer will stop. You then have five seconds to remove the bottle and close the case. Be precise. An ounce more or less will result in detonation. If you're still alive in five minutes, we'll speak again."

"Wait a second," McClane said.

Too late. Simon was gone.

The digital timer began counting down the seconds. McClane and Zeus each grabbed a jug . . . but what to do next? Five minutes was nothing. The timer was already at four minutes, fifty-seven seconds.

"I don't get it," said McClane. "You get it?"

"No."

"Obviously, we can't get four gallons in the three-gallon jug," said McClane, wishing he'd paid more attention in math class.

"Obviously."

"I know! Pour the three-gallon jug full, then pour it into the five. Now there's exactly three gallons in the five-gallon jug, right?" He stared at

Zeus, hoping his reasoning would stand up under scrutiny.

Zeus nodded. "Right. And then?"

"Fill the three-gallon jug a third of the way, giving us one more gallon." Yeah, but where did that leave them? Three-and-a-half minutes away from the eve of destruction, and he was fresh out of ideas. Maybe this was a sign from God that he should have stayed in LA.

"Shit! Every cop in fifty miles is chasing the biggest bomb threat in history, and I'm stuck here playing children's games!"

Zeus felt his rage boiling out of control. He was about to get his head blown off, all because this hotshot cop couldn't admit he was lost and ask for help. "You wanna try and focus on this for a minute?" he angrily demanded. "He said *exactly* four gallons. We can't eyeball the last gallon. Look, don't say you know unless you know. We have to be precise."

He took a deep breath and gave his mind a chance to clear. He was good at this shit. He could figure it out—if he stayed calm and McClane kept his mouth shut.

"What about a Coke bottle? That's it!" He snapped his fingers excitedly. "We get a sixteen-ounce coke bottle from the trash and fill the five-gallon bottle thirty-two times."

McClane scowled. "That's real fuckin' precise."

The timer on the scale was ticking down the seconds: 4:00, 3:59, 3:58 . . .

"I thought you were good at this shit." He glared at Zeus.

Zeus glared back at him. "I am. Stop fucking up my concentration. Okay, if we pour the three-gallon into the five-gallon . . ." He grabbed the five-gallon jug and shoved it under the water in the fountain.

"What are you doing?" McClane nervously demanded.

"I'm probably gettin' typhus and herpes from this shit. Kids piss in this thing." He removed the jug from the fountain and stuck it in front of McClane's face. "The five-gallon jug filled to the top. Exactly five gallons, right?"

"Right."

"Gimme the three-gallon."

McClane wasn't crazy about Zeus's attitude, but he figured this wasn't the best moment to remind him who was in charge. He dutifully did what Zeus had asked of him and watched as Zeus filled the empty three-gallon jug to the brim with water from the five-gallon.

Zeus held it up for both their inspection. "There were five gallons in here, but I poured off exactly three gallons into that jug, leaving me exactly two gallons in the five. Correct?"

"Okay," McClane said slowly, concentrating on Zeus's logic.

"Okay, watch."

Zeus emptied the three-gallon jug into the fountain. Next, he poured all the water that was left in the five-gallon jug into the three-gallon. "Exactly two gallons in the three-gallon, right? How much time?"

"Two and a half minutes," said McClane, trying to keep the tension out of his voice.

"Shit. Okay, okay. We fill the five back up." He resubmerged the larger jug in the fountain. "And then . . ." He sat back on his heels and stared at the two jugs.

McClane glared at him. "Do the rest!"

Zeus shook his head in defeat. "I don't know the rest of it," he said miserably.

"What? You were the one who said, 'Don't say anything unless you know it.' I thought *you* knew!" McClane screamed. He grabbed the handle of the three-gallon jug and tried to yank it away from Zeus.

"Let go," he ordered. "I'm starting over."

"We can't start over, McClane!" Zeus shouted.

The timer was down to a minute and fifty-eight seconds, and they were having a goddamn tug of war with a plastic jug. "Goddamn it!" yelled McClane. "Let go or I'll kick your ass to Harlem, you—"

He caught himself just in time and snapped his mouth closed.

"Go ahead, say it," Zeus said icily.

He felt ashamed. "What?" he said, trying to fake it.

"Nigger. You were gonna call me a nigger."

"I was not," McClane defended himself. "Asshole, maybe. What's your beef with white people, anyway? It's not like I own any slaves. My ancestors, to my knowledge, didn't own any slaves."

Zeus couldn't believe what he was hearing. "Jesus Christ! That is the stupidest—"

"You know what I think?" McClane broke in. "You're a racist!"

"Oh, Jesus Christ!"

"You don't like me because I'm white!"

"I don't like you because you're gonna get me killed!" Zeus yelled, clenching his fists to keep from taking a punch at the cop.

Simultaneously, they checked the timer, which showed 00:56.

"Shit, we've got under one minute!" Zeus said frantically. "Let's get rid of it!"

Smart move, cowboy. "Are you deaf? He said it'll detonate!" Determined to figure this one out, McClane stared at the two jugs. "Wait a minute, wait a minute . . . I got it!"

"You sure?"

He held up the three-gallon jug. "Watch. Exactly two gallons, right?"

Zeus nodded.

McClane set the smaller jug on the edge of the fountain and pulled the five-gallon jug out of the water. "Exactly five in here, right? If we pour this into that until it comes to the top . . ." He poured until the water brimmed to the top. ". . . we're left with exactly four gallons in the five-gallon jug!"

Zeus stared at the jugs in awed amazement. "You did it!" He slapped his hand against McClane's for a high five.

Their triumph was short-lived. Suddenly, they remembered that the bomb was still set to explode. The timer showed they had seven seconds left till detonation.

McClane grabbed the five-gallon jug and balanced it on the scale. They sighed a chorus of relief as the timer froze at five seconds. McClane slammed shut the briefcase and waited.

Four . . . three . . . two . . . one.

No blast. Only the normal, everyday sounds of the children shouting in the playground behind them, the water splashing in the fountain, the cars honking on the streets outside the park. They sank to their knees, as much to give thanks as to recover their equilibrium.

The phone rang.

"Yeah," said McClane. "We did it."

"You surprise me again, John. This could become an ugly habit." Simon laughed, sounding more bitter than amused.

"I got no time now, Simon. Deal's a deal," McClane reminded him. "The school bomb."

"But you have lots of time. Two hours, forty-seven minutes, to be precise. Plenty of time to test your wits again."

"Goddamn it, my wits are tired out! Where's the goddamn bomb?" screamed McClane, scaring awake an elderly Ukranian neighborhood lady on an nearby bench who'd nodded off in the sun.

"Temper, John," tsked Simon. "The path to truth has many turns. You'll find an envelope under the fountain. While taking the journey it suggests, ask yourself this: What is twenty-one out of forty-two?" He chuckled at his wit, then hung up abruptly.

McClane had no trouble finding Simon's envelope. He groaned when he saw what was inside. "He's sending us to the home-team dugout in Yankee Stadium. Why?"

"We're the home team," Zeus point out. "We supposed to find something there?"

"Maybe," said McClane. But Yankee Stadium was way the hell up in the Bronx, an hour's trip by subway, *if* they were lucky. And the question still remained: "What's twenty-one out of forty-two?"

"Leaves twenty-one again. Half of forty-two. But half a what?"

McClane mulled over the possibilities. "Could

be a person. Say there's forty-two players on the Yankees, one who wears number twenty-one. His name.'' He imagined the lineup, then shook his head. ''No. The squad's not that big.''

''Twenty-one's a game. Twenty-one's a club,'' said Zeus.

''It's a fucking goose chase is what it is!'' McClane said, slamming one of the jugs into the fountain.

Zeus threw him a dirty look, reminding him that neither one of them was there by choice. A goddamn psychopath was holding the city hostage, and it was up to them to put a stop to his game.

''Okay,'' he said, chastened. ''Fuck. Where's the nearest train?'' He pictured the subway map and came up with the Astor Place station on the Lexington Avenue line, three blocks away, which would take them straight to the Stadium.

About ten yards later, they were both struck with the same thought. They stopped to stare at the briefcase, still sitting on the fountain.

''I don't think we should leave that there,'' Zeus said.

McClane shook his head. ''Christ. I already did my subway with a bomb today.''

''Well, we can't leave it there. Some little kid could . . .''

He didn't have to say anymore than that before McClane nodded his agreement. While Zeus went back to retrieve the case, McClane noticed a deli across the street. He thought about cigarettes and beer and couldn't get there fast enough.

He was about to walk inside when a couple of kids streaked past him, their hands loaded with bags and bars of junk food. The shopkeeper rushed out after them, screaming for them to stop. The boys, neither of whom could have been older than twelve, jumped on their bikes to make their escape. McClane stuck out an arm and grabbed the nearer one by the collar.

"Lemme go, dickhead!" shrieked the kid.

"Watch your mouth!" McClane pulled the kid up off the bike. "What the hell's wrong with you? You wanna end up a juvie for some potato chips"—he squinted at the kid's loot and grimaced—"and Lumpy-loo bars?"

The kid grinned with the excitement of passing along a hot tip. "Look around, dude. The cops are all into something, charging around like crazy. Today's Christmas, man! You could steal city Hall!"

Yeah, thought McClane. The kid had a point. But who the hell would want to steal City Hall, except for the guy who'd lost it in the last election? He gazed off in the direction of Wall Street, concentrating so hard that he didn't notice Zeus had caught up with him. On the other hand, if you were looking for something worth stealing . . .

He let go of the kid and grabbed his bike. "C'mon on!" he called to Zeus.

Zeus didn't bother asking any questions. He yanked the other boy's bike away from him, jumped on, and pedaled down Avenue A after McClane.

"Hey! Those are our bikes!" screamed the boys.

"It's Christmas, right?" Zeus called over his shoulder. "Where you going?" he yelled to Mc-Clane, holding tight to the briefcase. "Yankee Stadium's the other way!"

The only explanation he got from McClane was, "Trust me!"

What a pal.

Chapter 7

They were back where they'd started, at the Wall Street blast site, quiet now except for a dump truck that almost creamed McClane as he biked into the square, and a trio of cops he didn't recognize.

"What the hell's wrong with you?" Zeus yelled, fuming because he'd had to be the one to carry the bomb over all those potholes.

McClane got straight to the point. "What is it Wall Street doesn't have?

"What? Is this catching? Now you're talking riddles?" Zeus shrugged. "Okay, I'll bite."

"Schools," said McClane. He shaded his eyes with his hand and stared up the block at the Federal Reserve Building. "And what is it they got loads of?" He was pretty sure he was right, but there was only one way to find out. He said, "I'll be back in a minute."

Zeus pointed to the briefcase. "Hey, what do I do with this?"

"Give it to those guys," said McClane, gesturing toward the cops guarding the crater.

"He's here," Rolf murmured into his radio.

Simon's voice crackled across the frequency. "Perhaps you could be more specific."

"McClane just showed up, and he's walking toward the bank. The black man is coming toward me," said Rolf.

"It's a pity. I was enjoying the idea of McClane spending the afternoon on the third base line," said Simon. He glanced over at Targo, in the driver's seat of the lead dump truck. "But so be it. May he rest in peace. I'll instruct Nigel. Pack up your team and get out."

"And the other one?" asked Rolf, as Zeus approached him. "I'm afraid I'll need an answer on that issue."

"Let him go," said Simon. The Good Samaritan had been sufficiently punished. His quarrel was with McClane.

"Understood," said Rolf. He turned off the radio and looked at Zeus. "Yes, sir?"

Zeus nodded at the three cops. "You guys better take this. Christ!" he said quickly, as one of them started to open the briefcase. "Don't open it! It's a bomb!"

"Another one? Oh, I see. We'll take care of

it.'' Rolf nodded, then turned to the other men. ''We have to move.''

Zeus stared after them as they headed for the unmarked gray car parked at the curb. They were the last three cops around. So why were they leaving? Something didn't feel right about this setup.

It felt even less right when the cop holding the briefcase put it down on the sidewalk before he got into the car.

Rolf felt the same way. ''What are you doing?'' he snapped at his colleague, whose name was Roman.

''I don't want to ride with it,'' the other man whined.

''Well, you can't leave it there. Some kid could . . .'' Rolf shook his head. Targo had drummed into their heads that the mission was about money, not murder. ''Put it in the backseat.''

Roman reluctantly did as he was told and got in the car.

Zeus watched the car pull away from the square. ''Hey!'' he shouted. ''You gonna leave this place unguarded?''

Three marshals were on duty in the lobby of the Federal Reserve Bank. McClane flipped his shield at the marshal seated behind the guard desk and identified himself. ''McClane, NYPD.''

Nigel, who'd been forewarned by Simon via

radio that McClane was on his way over, nodded hospitably. "What can I do for you, Lieutenant?"

"You have anything strange happen, say, in the last hour?" asked McClane.

"No, and we've had cops in here pretty steady since the subway thing. We were just gonna make a round on the vault floor," he said, coming out from behind the desk.

Maybe he'd guessed wrong. It had never happened before, but there had to be a first time, even for him. Still, he wanted to see for himself that everything was kosher. "Mind if I tag along?" he asked.

Nigel shrugged. "More the merrier."

McClane followed the marshal to an elevator, where three men—two more guards and an NYPD detective—were already waiting. The doors opened, and they all got in.

"Detective . . . Otto, isn't it?" Nigel said to the NYPD man. "Here's one of your guys. It's . . . ?"

"McClane. Major Crimes."

Otto grunted hello, and the elevator door slid shut.

"I keep telling myself to take the stairs, just for the exercise," Nigel said. "But it seems like I always wind up riding the lift."

Lift. McClane got stuck on the word. What was wrong with this picture?

He glanced at Detective Otto's badge, hanging from his breast pocket. Number 6911. Bingo! He had a winner. Same number that Walsh played every week in the lottery, 'cause like half the cops in New York City, he always played his badge number.

"Ever play the Lotto?" he asked. "My wife buys me two tickets every week. And it's always the same number. Only problem is, in ten years, I still haven't been able to figure *why* she buys that particular number. Damndest thing. Here, see if you can—"

He pretended to reach into his pocket for his tickets and closed his hand around his gun. The elevator was crowded. He was outnumbered, four to one, and they were all armed. Forget about pulling the gun out of its holster. This had to be quick and dirty and deadly.

He gently maneuvered the gun so it was facing sideways, pressed the trigger, and shot through his jacket, hitting the man on his left. A quarter-turn further left, and he got the guy behind him. He pinned the third phony marshal against the wall with his shoulder, then whipped out his gun and jammed it against Detective Otto's belly.

They were all four dead by the time the elevator doors opened. "In America it's called an elevator, shithead," he said, stepping over the phony desk guard's corpse.

He alternately trained his gun left and right as

he moved down the corridor that led to the vault. The place was as quiet as a graveyard. The monitor room was empty, the door to the vault itself wide open. Inside, seven federal marshals—*real* ones, he guessed them to be—lay unconscious on the floor.

The vault was empty. Nothing. Squat. Not a gold bar in sight. He moved further into the vault and discovered the hole that had been drilled in the wall.

"Hey! Anybody in there?" Zeus's voice floated toward him from somewhere in the distance.

He stepped through the hole and groped this way along the tunnel, until he found himself following the subway tracks.

"What the hell's going on?" asked Zeus, suddently emerging from the darkness.

"See for yourself." He pointed toward the vault and continued down the tracks, passing the discarded skidsteers. He saw the three bodies before he even reached the platform. He knew without looking that one of them was Walsh's.

"Aw, shit, Ricky," he muttered, kneeling to feel the pulse at Walsh's throat. He was a kid, just starting on his career. It shouldn't have ended for him like this.

He heard footsteps clattering along the tracks. His gun cocked, he whirled around. It was Zeus.

"Simon fucking says, I should've seen it a

mile off," he said bitterly. "It's not revenge. It's a fucking heist."

"What was in there?" asked Zeus.

McClane picked up a gold bar that lay on the platform. "This."

"Whooa!" Zeus hefted the bar with both hands. "This stuff's heavy. They cleaned out a whole room? It'd take a tank to move that. It'd take—"

"Dump trucks," said McClane, staring up at the ramp that stretched to the crater above them. "It'd take about fourteen great big dump trucks."

Like the one pulling out as they'd raced into the square on their bikes.

"It was heading east," said Zeus.

"Where you think you're going with that?" McClane pointed to the gold bar.

"It's only one!" Zeus clutched the gold against his chest as he scrambled up the ramp after McClane.

"They're not gonna let you keep that, Zeus."

"They owe me 'loss of livelihood compensation,' " Zeus said indignantly.

"Okay. But they're still not gonna let you keep it."

A cop was a cop, Zeus reminded himself. "We'll see."

The problem, once they emerged from the crater, was how to chase down the dump trucks. Forget the bikes. Simon's men had too big a jump on them. They needed a car, and the only candidate was a Yugo, parked just outside the square.

"Police authority?" asked Zeus.

McClane nodded. "Be my guest."

Zeus smashed the driver's side window with the gold bar, unlocked the front door, and slid inside. He tossed the gold bar onto the back seat and opened the other door for McClane. Then he pulled out the set of electrician's screwdrivers he always carried in his pocket.

"Can you hotwire this thing?" asked Mc-Clane.

" 'Course I can. I'm an electrician. Only problem is, it takes too fucking long." He winked at McClane and jammed a screwdriver into the ignition. The engine purred like a kitten. He shifted into first, floored the gas, and went hunting for Simon and his cohorts.

All that gold . . . They'd want to get it offshore as quickly as possibly, but how? They certainly couldn't airlift a load that size out of the country. The Canadian and Mexican borders were too far away for a convoy of dump trucks to elude apprehension. But a ship, docked within easy driving distance, could not only carry the weight of the gold, but also reach international waters well before the three o'clock deadline.

The dump trucks had been headed in the wrong direction for the New Jersey ports across the

Hudson River. McClane's first best guess were the old Brooklyn Navy Yards.

They shot up the ramp to the Brooklyn Bridge and pulled over to scan the traffic flowing into Brooklyn. For as far as McClane could see, there was a steady flow of cars, motorcyles, and vans, but not a dump truck in sight.

"Nothing on the bridge," he said glumly.

"McClane!" Zeus grabbed his arm and pointed toward the FDR Drive, just to their left. A line of dump trucks snaked north, the last one only about two miles away.

"Go! Go! Go!" McClane urged, as they roared onto the FDR. He pulled out his cellular phone and scowled at the mangled mess of plastic. "Ah, fuck."

"What?"

"I shot the phone," he said. He tossed it into the backseat and stared through the windshield, mentally urging Zeus to hurry up. He wished he were the one in the driver's seat. Not that Zeus wasn't doing a good job. They were zipping in and out of the left lane, passing the slower-moving vehicles, gaining on the trucks. They couldn't be more than half a mile ahead now. But the tension was killing him. He kept seeing Walsh, lying on the subway Platform with a blood-soaked bullet hole in the middle of his chest.

"Okay." Zeus prompted him. "Twenty-one out of forty-two?"

He shook his head. "Not a clue."

"What about Yankee Stadium?"

"We'll get there! But that son-of-a-bitch isn't getting off Manhattan," he said, as a woman driver cut them off and zoomed past.

"Jesus Christ!" He stuck his head out the window and yelled, "Who do you think you are, Hillary Clinton?"

"That's it!" Zeus shouted.

"What?"

"Hillary Clinton. The forty-second president!"

What a nightmare. McClane rolled his eyes in disgust. "No. She would be the forty-third."

Zeus glared at McClane. Since when was it his job to figure out Simon's goddamn riddles? "Fine," he challenged the cop. "So who was the twenty-first?"

"I don't know."

"You don't?"

McClane sighed. "No. Do you?"

"No."

McClane decided it was time to change the subject. "What kind of engine does this piece-of-shit have?"

"It's a Yugo. Built for economy, not speed."

"Next time, steal American!" McClane snapped. He deliberately turned his back on Zeus and stared covetously at a Mercedes gliding past them, driven by some greasy-haired yuppie-law-yer type, who was yakking on his cellular phone.

Say goodbye, scumball. He grabbed the steer-ing wheel, yanked the car to the right, and cut off the Mercedes, forcing the driver to pull over into the breakdown lane.

"What are you doing?" Zeus screamed.

"Getting a phone," said McClane. He hopped out of the car, pulled out his detective's shield, and went to give the yuppie the bad news.

Three minutes later, the yuppie stood glaring at them as the Mercedes screeched onto the FDR with McClane in the driver's seat. Egged on by McClane, Zeus suddenly rolled down the window and called, "Hey! Who was the twenty-first pres-ident?"

"Go fuck yourself!" shouted the outraged yuppie.

"That guy was pissed," said Zeus, watching in the sideview mirror as the yuppie hammered his fists against the hood of the Yugo.

"He'll feel better when he looks in the back seat," McClane said, dialing 911.

It took a couple of seconds for the realization to hit Zeus. Then, "Goddamn it! That was my gold bar!"

The phone rang twice before a recording came on the line. "At this moment, the emergency switchboard is busy . . ." But suddenly, there was a human voice at the other end. "Police dispatch. Yes?"

"This is McClane. Get me Walter Cobb."

The reception temporarily faded as the road passed under a building that straddled the Drive. When he came out the other side, Cobb was yelling, "John? Where the hell are you?"

"Walter," he shouted into the phone. "It's not a revenge! It's a heist!"

"What??"

"They knocked over the Federal Reserve. They got gold. A shitload of it! They're headed north in dump trucks."

"Are you drinking again, McClane?"

"Not since breakfast. There's a line of dump trucks northbound on the FDR at about Seventieth Street. You gotta close the bridges and get a chopper over there."

"I couldn't close a hot dog stand right now!" Cobb shouted. "We're spread all over hell! What about the damn bomb?"

"Find out who the twenty-first president was. It's got something to do with it," McClane said, as the road passed under another building. "Walter?" he yelled. "Walter? Ah, fuck!"

He slammed the phone onto the seat. He'd lost the reception. Walter was gone.

Across town, in the makeshift command center that had been set up in a West Side high school basement, Cobb was still trying to figure out the end of McClane's question. "John? John?" he bellowed into the phone. "The twenty-first what?"

Static crackled in his ear. He gave up in disgust and focused on what McClane had just told him. It was wacky, but so was Simon wacky, and McClane had, in fact, sounded stone-cold sober. He couldn't afford not to believe him—just in case he was right.

"Get hold of Munson at Triboro," he said to Kowalski. "Tell him to close the East River bridges north of Fifty-ninth. He's looking for dump trucks."

"Dump trucks?"

"He says there's a bunch of dump trucks going up the FDR loaded with gold."

"Walter," said Kowalski. "They don't allow dump trucks on the FDR."

Like he didn't know that. "Connie!" he barked. He pitied her husband.

"All right, you don't want me to argue, I won't argue. No matter how stupid it is!" she said.

He watched her a second to make sure she was dialing the Triboro's number. And thought, *Women!*

Katya had been nervously waiting for Simon and Targo at their Central Park Reservoir meeting point. In her running shoes, shorts, and T-shirt,

she easily blended in with the other women running the mile-and-a-half loop that circled the reservoir. She'd jogged back and forth along the dirt
path, all the while keeping a sharp eye out for the
trucks. When the first one finally appeared on the
flat ground just below the track, she rushed to
meet it and flew into Targo's arms.

She knew he disapproved when she allowed
her feelings for him to show, especially when
they were working together on a job. Mercenaries
were supposed to be tough. Unemotional. Invin-
cible. But they'd both had so many close calls,
been so often claimed for dead by their enemies,
that sometimes she couldn't contain herself.

He hustled her into the cab of the truck without
so much as a kiss and immediately got back to
the business at hand.

"The men at the stadium? Stay or go?" he
asked Simon.

Simon glanced at his watch as he dialed the
number of the guard desk at the Federal Reserve
Bank on his cellular phone. "Nigel should have
checked in by now."

He counted fifteen unanswered rings before he
hung up. Nigel wasn't answering. Something was
wrong. Was it possible that McClane had eluded
the men who'd been stationed at the bank? He
frowned and turned back to Targo.

"Keep them there," he said. "McClane may
still be alive."

Targo glared at him accusingly, not needing words to express what he was thinking.

"Stop," said Simon. "If he's alive, he won't be talking to anyone."

He smiled as he punched more numbers on his phone. The game was about to become even more amusing.

"K-Rock, the Flash."

The disc jockey's brash, high-octane delivery grated on Simon's nerves. But the consequences of his conversation with the Flash—who had the number-one rating in the midday time slot for the tri-state region—would be well worth his momentary discomfort.

"You're on the air. What's up?" said the Flash.

Simon imagined the bored radio deejay stuck in the sound booth, his feet propped up on the desk, waiting for his shift to end. He mentally fished for a suitable accent and decided on Brooklyn. Nasal, slightly slurred, a guy who worked with his hands, a union man, probably Irish. "I just wanted to tell you what a great show ya got. I listen to ya all the time and—"

The deejay cut him off. "Thank you. We try. What was it you wanted to say?"

Rude bastard, thought Simon. Aloud, he said, "Well, ya know all those cop cars screamin' around everywhere? Know what they're up to?" He waited a beat to build the suspense. He could hear the deejay breathing at the other end. He could feel him wondering, was this guy for real?

"There's a bomb in a school. My cousin's a cop. Somebody put a really big bomb in a school somewhere. Only they don't know which, so they're searching *all* of 'em. *Every school in the metropolitan area.*"

The Flash, the essence of hip, lost his cool. "Holy shit!" he said, as all over New York, his listeners dropped whatever they were doing and rushed to their phones.

At Emergency Police Dispatch, Wanda Shepherd tore into yet another pack of cigarettes and glared at the switchboard, which was ringing out of control. "Turley!" she shrieked. "Everyone in the goddamn city just called 911!"

"They're gone," said Zeus.

Balancing one hand on the wheel, McClane half-shoved himself out the window to get a better look at the road ahead. He'd lost them at Fifty-ninth Street when he got stuck under the bridge. Zeus was right. It was as if a magician had snapped his fingers and made the trucks disappear from the FDR.

"Fuckin' David Copperfield," he muttered. He retrieved the phone, dialed 911, and got a strange-sounding busy signal. "Shit!" He had to get through to Cobb and alert him. The trucks must have exited at Seventy-ninth Street. They had to be heading for the Bronx.

"There! Down there!" yelled Zeus.

McClane peered over the Drive and saw a lone dump truck, traveling west. "This thing have airbags?" he asked.

"Your side does, I don't know about mine. Why?"

McClane's answer was graphic and dramatic. With no further warning, he accelerated to the max and blasted through the guardrail. Twin airbags erupted in their faces like giant helium balloons. McClane held tight to the wheel, struggling to see over the top of the bag as the car plummeted eight or ten feet to the street below.

It hit the pavement with a bone-rattling succession of jolts and bounces that battered his spine all the way up into his skull. He hurt like hell, but the pain was reassuring. The lack of it could mean he was eligible to spend the rest of his life in a wheelchair. He wiggled his arms and legs to make sure everything was properly functioning and silently vowed to buy a Mercedes next time he went car-shopping. Any other make, they would have been dead on impact.

The airbags began to deflate. He suddenly realized that he and Zeus were both coated in a white, flour-like substance that had to be some kind of baking soda-based flame retardant.

"You look like a ghost!" Zeus said, his teeth still chattering with fright.

Maybe he was a ghost, come back from the grave to haunt Simon. He grinned as he brushed the white powder out of his eyes. "You look like Al Jolson inside out!" he chortled.

Zeus managed a weak yuck. He was alive. So was McClane. Had to be some Higher Power watching over them. Otherwise, they'd both be dead for sure.

The Mercedes was listing to the left, and there was a long jagged crack in the middle of the windshield, but it was still in one piece, and it was running. The dump truck had a four-block advantage, but the driver was sticking to the speed limit, tooling along East Eight-sixth Street as if he had all the time in the world.

McClane whipped across the broad, well-traveled cross-street, dodging slow-moving buses that stopped at every corner, and jaywalkers intent on playing chicken with the two-way flow of traffic. He figured the truck was headed for the road that transversed the park at Eighty-fifth Street. Sure enough, its left-turn signal began to blink as it slowed for the light at Fifth Avenue.

A mob of preppie high-school boys sauntered across Madison Avenue, dribbling basketballs as if they owned the street. He pounded the horn, and one of them flashed him the finger. Any other time, he would have nabbed the kid for harrassing a police officer. Now, instead, he gritted his teeth until they passed, then zipped through the intersection.

He finally caught up with the truck just as the driver was about to hit Fifth. Swerving right to block it from turning, he slammed on his brakes and flew out of the car with his gun drawn.

He rushed toward the truck, screaming, "Get out with your hands up!"

There was no one in the front seat. Shit. Not even Simon could program a truck to drive itself. He kept his gun aimed at the seat and yanked open the door. Oh, yeah, there was a driver, all right. He was crouched on the floor with his hands raised above his head, cowering with fear. McClane glared at him. If he was a terrorist-for-hire, then Simon ought to be rethinking his recruitment policy.

"Don't kill me!" pleaded the driver.

"Get out!" McClane ordered. Keeping his gun trained on the man, and went to check the back of the truck. Except for a crumpled coffee cup, it was empty.

Great. He'd almost killed himself and Zeus and wasted ten precious minutes following the wrong goddamn dump truck. He put his gun away and showed the driver his shield. "Where're you going?" he asked.

"The aqueduct," the man said, slowly lowering his hands and pulling himself up off the floor.

"The aqueduct?"

The driver pointed toward Central Park. "The new aqueduct."

"Show me," said McClane. He hopped on the running board for the brief ride into the park and over to the reservoir, while Zeus trailed them in the Mercedes.

The driver pulled onto the service road and continued on until they came to the edge of a gaping hole next to an enormous mound of dirt about halfway along the eastern side of the reservoir. A huge pipe, at least thirty feet in diameter, stretched from the mouth of the excavation into the ground beneath the reservoir. Six dump trucks waited in line next to the mountain of dirt.

"See?" said the driver. "Goes from here all the way to the Catskills."

McClane shook his head. "What does?"

"That! The water pipe! Goes for sixty miles."

A man in a hard hat was waving a telephone and yelling orders at a crane operator. McClane guessed he was the foreman and went over to question him. "You get, like, any extra trucks through here in the last few minutes?" he asked as Zeus came up to join him.

The hard hat mopped his brow with a stained bandanna and spat on the ground. "I'm gonna write these clowns up," he said angrily. "They don't start paying attention to the work orders, I'm gonna—"

McClane held up a hand. "Whoa! Who?"

"The dozen idiots who tore ass up there." The foreman pointed to the pipe. "We're not loading up there anymore. We're loading here!"

Score a point for Simon. "So much for bridges and helicopters," he grunted. He flipped his shield at the foreman, borrowed his phone, and dialed 911. It was busy. "You got a map?" he asked.

The foreman nodded. The Central Park Reservoir, which used to supply much of New York's drinking water, was fed by rain and spring runoff from the snow-covered Catskill Mountains. The reservoir was connected to the watershed area by an elaborate system of underground tunnels. A chart of the system was spread out on a table.

"We run pretty much under the Saw Mill until you get up to the cofferdam," said the foreman, tracing the route for him on the map. "From there on, we've already brought the water down from the reservoir. But the cofferdam holds it . . . here."

"Is there another way in or out?"

"Well, there's a vent shaft every two miles."

"No. With a truck." He tried 911 again. Still busy. "Shit!" At this rate, he would never get through to Cobb.

"You can get a truck out at the cofferdam," the foreman said. "You can get there on the surface. Just follow the Saw Mill Parkway. It's maybe twenty miles.''

''I'll meet you there,'' McClane told Zeus, pointing on the map to the exit that the foreman had showed him. ''I'm goin' after them.''

''Wait!'' Zeus said. ''What am I gonna do?''

Only one thing for him to do. ''Go to Yankee Stadium,'' he said, sprinting toward the truck.

Yankee Stadium? And what the hell was he supposed to do once he got there? He watched the dump truck tear out of the park and said, ''Goddamn it, McClane!''

Chapter 8

McClane made himself comfortable and watched the driver maneuver the truck past the pipe into the aqueduct. "What's your name?" he said, making conversation.

"Jerry Parks," said the driver.

"Nice to meet you," he said companionably. "This is a pretty big water pipe, Jerry."

Jerry nodded enthusiastically. "Thirty-two feet in diameter. Forty-six million cubic feet of rock moved so far. You know, that's ten times the Hoover Dam. In a minute, there'll be five hundred sixteen feet of rock between us and the surface. This part is phase three of Tunnel three. Planning for it started back in 1954, but construction didn't begin until June of 'Seventy. You know what the most interesting thing about Tunnel three is?"

Yakety yak. He was stuck in a long dark tube

with Chatty Charlie. ''No, Jerry,'' he said, almost afraid to ask. ''What?''

''The valves. Each one is located in a separate housing chamber for easier access, which is a pretty big design departure from Tunnels One and Two.''

McClane nodded mechanically, but his mind was on Simon and the gold. The Saw Mill ended abruptly somewhere in the middle of northern Westchester County. Where was Simon headed from there? He stared through the windshield into the darkness of the tunnel and tried to put himself in Simon's place. Further upstate were mostly small manufacturing towns and dairy farms that were dying a slow death. Secrets were hard to keep in such places, and outsiders were eyed with suspicion. He'd be crazy to roll through there with all that gold.

They rounded a corner, and the gleam of tail lights up from a truck parked up ahead brought him back to the present. ''Hold it, Jerry,'' he said.

Maybe his luck was changing. Or maybe the driver was one of Jerry's pals from the reservoir. Either way, it was worth a quick look. ''Give me your hat,'' he said. ''Wait here.''

He pulled the hard hat low over his face and walked over to the parked truck. ''Hey, there!'' he said, eyeing the two men inside. ''Mickey O'Brien, fellas, treasurer, Teamsters Union Local

Three-seventeen. I'm up for reelection, and I thought I'd come down here to press the flesh.''

There was a glint of steel as the driver raised his hand to window-level. McClane grabbed for his gun and fired two shots through the door. The driver slumped onto the wheel; his passenger toppled over against the side window. So much for pressing their flesh.

The driver's body tumbled onto the pavement when McClane opened the door to the truck. He squatted beside it and checked the guy's pockets. "Show me something, dickhead," he muttered.

There wasn't much to see: a driver's license, a Teamster's card, both of them no doubt phony. A pack of Marlboros, matches, and ten quarters, neatly wrapped in clear cellophane.

McClane lit up one of the cigarettes and contemplated the roll of quarters.

"Holy shit!" Jerry, looking a little queasy, had come up behind him. "That guy's dead."

"Yep." McClane drew on the cigarette, enjoying the taste of it in his mouth. He said, "Jerry, I want you to get hold of a cop named Cobb. He's the head of my unit. Call him, find him, track him down. Tell him where I went."

Jerry couldn't seem to tear his gaze away from the terrorist's body. He nodded yes, he understood.

"And tell him to find out who the twenty-first

president was. The bomb's got something to do with that."

"Chester A. Arthur," said Jerry.

"Chester A. Arthur?"

"Yeah, Chester A. Arthur, 1881–1885. Nominated vice president in 1880, succeeded to the presidency on Garfield's death six months later. Interesting man. Did you know he was a collector of customs right here in New York?"

Jerry could make a killing on Jeopardy.

"No, I didn't know that," McClane said. He slid across the seat, opened the passenger side door, and shoved the other body out of the truck. Then he keyed the ignition, waved a jaunty goodbye to Jerry, and sped off in blessed silence down the tunnel.

Zeus was a Mets fan. He hated the American League, hated George Steinbrenner, hated the Yankees for all their puffed-up mythology about yesterday's heroes. The Mets were about what was happenin' *now*: scrappy play, bad-ass attitude. Yankee Stadium was a monument to a dying era stuck in a decaying corner of the southwest Bronx.

The team was on the road today, and the place looked deserted. He darted past the landmark Big Bat at the main entrance, jumped over a turnstile, and hurried through the gate. The stadium field, vast and empty and silent, shimmered under the noonday sun. If terrorists were waiting to pounce on him, they were maintaining a low profile. To be safe, he did the same, keeping his head down as he crept along the perimeter of the diamond toward the home-team dugout.

Despite his caution, he was easily spotted by Erik and Jurgen, two of Simon's lieutenants, who stood hidden in the shadows, their guns and innoculators at the ready.

"The African is here," Erik quietly informed Simon on the CB.

Simon's truck, still at the head of the convoy, was just about to approach the cofferdam, the steel-and-timber retaining wall that prevented the water on the other side from flowing into the tunnel. A steel plate bridged an electrical trench in the tunnel's concrete floor. Simon waited until the last of the trucks had rumbled across the steel plate, then gave the signal that sent it tumbling into the trench.

As Targo drove the truck up the ramp that led to the surface, Simon said, "Alone. Are you certain?"

"Just the one," said Erik, watching Zeus pick up the small, plastic tiltball game Erik had left for him to find on the dugout bench.

Zeus turned the game over and saw the note taped to the bottom. GAME OVER, it read.

"Should we proceed?" asked Erik, as Zeus's eyes widened with bewilderment.

"No." Simon frowned. Why was Zeus alone? Where was the policeman? "Follow him to McClane. Then kill them both."

With a shake of his head, Erik tacitly conveyed Simon's command to Jurgen. A few feet away, unaware that he was being observed, Zeus glanced about apprehensively. If the game was over, what happened next? A *Wizard of Oz*-like appearance by Simon at home plate? A home-run bomb rocketing over the outfield wall?

A slight breeze ruffled the grass. A jet roared by overhead. Otherwise, all was still and quiet at the House that Ruth Built.

"Where is he?" Targo demanded.

Simon ignored him and changed channels on his CB. "You can come along now, Nils," he said into the radio. Impatient for a response, he repeated himself. "Nils?"

"Nils is dead, fuckhead," came McClane's voice. "So's his pal."

His worst fears about to be realized, Targo glared at Simon as McClane gave them a body count. "And four other guys from the East German All-Star Team. Your boys at the bank are gonna be late. Forever."

Simon's jaw twitched with suppressed rage, but his calm, quiet tone betrayed not a hint of tension. A professional knew how and when to adjust the plan, to improvise, even compromise, if absolutely necessary. "The truck you're driving contains thirteen billion dollars in gold bullion. Let's not be rash, John. Would a deal be out of the question?"

"Sure," said McClane.

Simon looked gloatingly at Targo.

"Simon?" said McClane. "How about you get out and bend over and I'll drive this truck up your ass?"

"How very colorful," Simon said, his cheeks mottled with red.

"Yippee-kye-ay, motherfucker," yelled McClane.

This time, *he* got to be the one who hung up first.

"I told you not to toy with this man," Targo rebuked Simon.

Simon felt the peculiar telltale throbbing in his temple that meant a migraine was about to come on. He dug in his pocket for his prescription headache pills and gulped down a handful. "Thank you, Mathias. That's very helpful."

They reached the surface of the aqueduct exit. Targo pulled the truck over as the rest of the convoy continued past them. A gray car was parked on the shoulder; Rolf and the other two phony cops from the Wall Street bomb site were waiting inside.

Armed with a machine gun, Targo jumped out of the truck. "Your game with the policeman has gone on long enough. You jeopardize the mission. That is not acceptable. We must kill him. Now,'' he said.

Simon sighed as he, too, climbed out of the truck. ''Yes, very well,'' he conceded.

Targo and the three phony cops, all of them carrying machine guns, started back down the ramp to the aqueduct.

Simon's gaze fell on a familiar item in the back seat of the grey car. ''Stop!'' he yelled.

Targo wheeled around. His tolerance for Simon was running thin. He was ready for a fight.

Simon smiled as he handed him the bomb that McClane and Zeus had retrieved from Tompkins Square Park. ''Blow the wall,'' he said.

Caught by surprise, Targo exclaimed, ''What?''

''I think you heard me.''

A rare grin lit up Targo's normally somber face. He grabbed the bomb from his partner's hand and ran for the cofferdam.

McClane entertained himself with images of what he would do to Simon when they finally met face-to-face. Based on what the foreman back at the reservoir had told him, he figured it wouldn't be too long now before he reached the cofferdam, where Simon would have had to exit the tunnel. By his calculations, the trucks couldn't have traveled very far beyond there yet.

He was still working on the question of how Simon was planning to get the gold out of the country. The Hudson River lay just to the west, but it hadn't seen any heavy shipping in years. Process of elimination led him east to Connecticut. Just one small problem, however, before he could give any more thought to Simon's escape route.

He braked to an abrupt stop just in time to avoid diving into the open trench that yawned in front of him. The truck would never make it across. But the rest of the convoy had passed this way. There had to be some sort of plank or plate that had been deliberately discarded after the last of Simon's trucks had made it over the trench.

He got out of the truck, slammed the door shut, and went to investigate. The sound echoed around him with a dull thud. Moments later, another, somewhat louder thud reverberated through the tunnel . . . except this one sounded more like a boom.

Great. He was hearing things. It figured, after the beating his body had taken this morning.

Just as he'd guessed, the steel plate that usually bridged the trench lay on the bottom. He hopped over the edge and tried to pry it out. But the sucker was wedged sideways, and he couldn't budge it. He dropped to one knee, hove his shoulder up under it, and tried to get some leverage.

His concentration was interrupted by a muffled

clap of thunder. Except, he suddenly realized, he was too far underground to be hearing thunder. Anyway, the last he'd looked, the sun was shining and there wasn't a cloud in the sky. He decided he'd better check it out. He climbed out the far side of the trench and took a few steps down the tunnel in the direction of the noise.

Now, it was sounding more like running water. A lot of running water. Getting louder now. And darker. Like the darkness before a storm. He stared down the long, empty tunnel, lit from above by ceiling lights that seemed to stretch to infinity . . . lights that were suddenly, one by one, winking out.

Something weird was going on. He didn't know what it was, but he had a real strong sense that he shouldn't stick around to find out. He headed back to the truck, stopping just long enough to take another look over his shoulder. For the first time in years, he thought about a trip he and Holly had once had taken to Niagara Falls. He could still remember the thunderous roar of the falls, almost deafening in its intensity. He was hearing that same roar now, the sound of water moving at tremendous speed.

Goaded by instinct, he leaped over the trench and sprinted for the truck. As he scrambled into the cab, he caught a glimpse of the source of the noise: a thirty-foot wall of water cannonballing through the tunnel straight in his direction.

He frantically ground the gears and maneuvered the quickest five-point turn in history. He floored the gas and gunned the truck back down the tunnel. He was galloping, pushing forty miles an hour. But the truck was no match for the force of nature barreling toward him.

The water crashed into the truck with an awesome tornado-like force. McClane was thrown flat against the roof of the cab, as the truck was scooped up and flung across the water's surface like a surfboard balancing on the edge of a tidal wave.

His two choices were crystal clear. Escape or die. For the last couple of months, he'd been slowly drinking himself to death. But drowning his sorrows in booze was one thing; meeting his Maker in this washing machine from hell was a whole other ball game.

The truck had righted itself now. It was time to bail out. He dove through the window and hauled himself onto the roof of the truck. The wall of water had to be moving at seventy miles an hour, at least, plunging through the tunnel like a runaway train. He peered into the darkness, straining to see what lay ahead. Suddenly, he found salvation: Shafts of sunlight falling like spears through a ventilation grate above.

It was a long shot, but it was his only chance for escape. He was almost even with the light. He braced himself on top of the truck, threw up his arms, and flung himself at the grate. His fingers closed around the bars just as the truck tumbled away beneath him. The grate hinged backwards and sent him slamming into the roof of the tunnel. A swell of water swirled up and around him, threatening to drag him down into its vortex. Summoning a strength he didn't know he possessed, he held tight and clambered hand over hand, one agonizingly slow bar after another, toward the sunlight.

He just finally reached the surface when he was swept up into a surging column of water which sent him spinning high into the air above the open shaft. He landed on his ass, amid a shower of cold, muddy water.

He scrambled to get out of its way. A Mercedes came zooming up alongside him. "Jesus!" Zeus started at him through the car window. "You look like you been dipped in shit!"

In the words of the great Yogi Berra, he was having déjà vu all over again. First, an evening of hide-and-seek with Hans Gruber in Nakatomi Tower. Next, on yet another Christmas Eve, a snowball fight at Dulles Airport with a power-crazed U.S. Army colonel who had drugs on the brain. And now, a tag-team treasure hunt with Gruber's brother.

But like he'd said that night at Dulles, he didn't like to lose.

He stumbled over to the car. "How'd you find me?" he gasped.

"Real fuckin' difficult," said Zeus, eyeing the tower of water pouring out of the ventilation shaft.

"I thought you went to Yankee Stadium," McClane said grumpily.

"I did. This was on the bench. It's a fucking joke." Zeus tossed him the plastic game. McClane turned it over and stared at the message tape to the bottom: GAME OVER.

"No, it ain't," he said. "Something was supposed to happen."

"Well, nothing did. There wasn't anybody there."

"Someone *was* there."

"I'm telling ya," Zeus insisted. "He's jerking us off!"

A burst of bullets suddenly tore up the mud around him. More bullets slammed into the trunk of the Mercedes.

"Jesus Christ!" Zeus yelled.

McClane dove through the passenger's window. "Those guys who weren't at the stadium? They didn't follow you! Go! Go!"

Its siren wailing at full blast, Cobb's car screeched to a stop behind the Chester A. Arthur Elementary School. A large, noisy crowd was screaming at the police as Cobb emerged from the car, along with Jerry Park, Charlie Weiss, and Cobb's secretary. "Christ!" Cobb said, watching the irate parents try to surge past the barricades. "I thought we were going in the back way!"

"This *is* the back way, Walter," said Kowalski, who'd been waiting outside to escort him to the principal's office. "In half an hour, we'll have a riot in front of every school in the city!"

Cobb was met there by a squad of uniformed cops. "Start at the top floor," he said, getting right down to business. "Twenty men to a floor. Send the other fifty down to the basement with us." He turned to Jane and asked, "What about McClane?"

She shook her head. "No word. Westchester's trying to get people out to the aqueduct, but if anything, they're in worse shape than we are."

"This is kind of putting all our eggs in one basket, isn't it?" Weiss broke in. "Suppose McClane's wrong?"

Lambert rushed into the office, accompanied by a tiny, gray-haired woman. "Walter, this is the principal, Mrs. Martinez," he said.

Cobb saw the worry in the principal's eyes and wished he could say something to allay her fears. He needed her help to keep the children calm while the search was conducted. He knew that was asking a lot of her, but from the set of her jaw, he would bet she was up to the job.

"How do you do, Mrs. Martinez," he said. "A

large number of police will be coming into the
building in a few minutes. I'd like you to gather
your children in the auditorium.''

The principal nodded and hurried off to notify
her teachers.

Cobb hoped he wasn't making a mistake by
putting so much faith in the message he'd gotten
from McClane through Jerry Parks. Weiss was
right; they *were* putting all their eggs in one basket. But they had nothing else to go on. And Mc-
Clane, that goddamn pain in the ass, was more
often right than wrong.

The Saw Mill Parkway had been designed for lei-
surely drives in the country, for sightseeing and
pleasure trips. A narrow, twisting road that was
overhung with trees, its two well-trafficked northbound lanes were separated from the southbound
by a low metal railing that allowed very little
room to spare on either side. It was just the kind
of road that wasn't meant for outracing a bunch
of would-be assassins.

Zeus was doing his best to pick up speed and
stay in his lane as the road snaked around the
curves and a steady hail of bullets battered the
Mercedes. The rear window blew out, sending
splinters of glass flying all around them.

McClane whirled around and peered over the
back seat. A Dodge pickup was fast closing in on
them. He whipped out his gun, aimed, and emp-

tied the magazine at the pickup. A couple of shots
fell short, but the rest splattered against its grill.
The pickup swerved and fell back a short distance.

McClane reloaded the gun, swearing as the
Mercedes veered into the left lane and almost
crashed into the barrier. The pickup had gained
on them again and was angling to pull alongside
them to the right.

"Outta the way!" Zeus yelled at the slow-
moving Explorer that was riding in front of them.

"Go around him!" screamed McClane as Zeus
ponded the horn.

Another volley of bullets hit the back seat. Mc-
Clane grabbed the wheel and jerked the car to
the right of the Explorer, grinding its side. The
Explorer spun out of control in front of the
pickup. The pickup jumped the almost nonexis-
tent shoulder, slid past the Explorer, and was
back on their tail again.

"Go faster!" McClane bellowed.

"I am!"

McClane slapped another magazine into his
gun. "I found out who the twenty-first president
was," he said, getting ready to fire. "A guy
named Arthur."

"What?" Zeus shrieked. "The Chester A. Arthur Elementary School?"

He slammed on the brakes. The car bucked forward and began to slow up.

Before the pickup could gain the advantage, McClane shoved his foot on the gas. "What the fuck are you doing?" he shouted.

"My brother's kids are in that school!"

The Mercedes was swerving all over the highway, taking up both lanes. Zeus's momentary hesitation had given the pickup a chance to catch up with them. It rammed the back end of the Mercedes, and more shots whistled past their heads.

"Fuck!" yelled Zeus.

"Lemme drive!" McClane demanded. "Go over the seat!"

Zeus flopped over into the back as McClane slid behind the wheel. "Goddamn it!" he yelled. "Why didn't you tell me before? 'Course the bomb's in their school! He put it there on purpose!"

"Why the fuck would he do that?"

Was Zeus stupid or what? "To make sure he had your complete attention!" McClane snapped. He sped up and kept his eye on the road. He lurched around a curve, barely missing the shoulder, and swung across the right lane into the left.

The pickup had fallen out of sight. Zeus climbed back into the passenger seat. "We gotta go back!" he announced.

"What're you gonna do? Stand there and watch it go off? Fuck that. We gotta get to Simon!"

"I can't leave those kids, goddamn it!"

McClane rolled his eyes. "Let your brother stand there with his thumb up his ass!"

"He can't, McClane! Some white cop killed him!"

Before McClane had a chance to ask how, Zeus supplied the answer. "In a crackhouse, in a fucked-up raid."

"If he was on crack, his life was already in the toilet."

"Fuck you! He hated drugs. He had a family. A business. He was the squarest man you ever met."

The pickup was right behind them again. McClane pressed his foot flat on the gas. The car was traveling as fast as he could get it to move.

"Then what the hell was he doing there?" he demanded.

"Trying to take *me* home!"

McClane stared at him in stunned silence. "Jesus," he muttered.

Wham! The pickup screeched around the corner, smashed into their rear fender, and sent them flying across the highway. The driver drew parallel to them. Another man leaned out the window and pointed an MP-5 machine gun.

"Get down!" screamed McClane.

Zeus ducked. Machine gun fire raked the Mercedes. McClane lowered his head. The car swung out of control and swerved from lane to lane. A storm of bullets chewed up its roof, along with the interior. The other cars slid onto the shoulder to get out of their way.

They were covered in pieces of plastic, glass, and leather. A bullet scraped Zeus's neck. Another sliced through McClane's arm.

"Jesus Christ! Jesus Christ!" Zeus screamed over and over again.

The barrage stopped abruptly. The pickup fell back. McClane guessed that the shooter had to reload. "Where's the fuse panel?" he yelled.

Zeus's hand was shaking as he pointed to a spot under the dashboard. "There."

"Pull the antilock brakes," McClane said.

"I don't know which—"

"Then pull them all!" he yelled. "Get down on the floor! Way down! This is gonna get ugly!"

He checked his gun. He kept one foot on the gas and readied the other over the brake. He watched the rear view mirror as the pickup tightened the gap between them again.

"Your nephews aren't gonna die. You hear me? That bomb ain't going off! We're gonna find Simon and rip the fucking code out of his throat if we have to!" he said.

The pickup accelerated. McClane bided his time. He was waiting for them. Waiting for that one sweet, perfect moment. The shooter leaned out the window, ready to finish them off.

McClane stabbed the brakes, cranked the wheel, and threw the car into neutral. Doing eighty miles an hour, it spun around backwards and brought them face to face with the pickup cab. The two terrorists gawked at him. McClane stuck his gun out the window. He and the shooter both opened fire. Bullets ripped through the air in a lightning roll of gunfire.

The Mercedes slid past the pickup. McClane kept firing. He got a quick glance at the cab, saw an explosion of blood and glass. The pickup spun off the road. McClane swerved to avoid it and lost control of the car. The Mercedes flipped sideways, rolled over and down the embankment, and slid to a stop on its roof.

Zeus opened his eyes and looked up at the floor of the car. "What happened?" he asked.

McClane struggled to free himself from his seat belt. "Got your Triple-A card?" he said.

They quickly extricated themselves from the Mercedes and cautiously approached the pickup truck. McClane lowered his gun after a glance through the shattered windshield. The shooter was sprawled against the seat with half his face blown off. The driver was lying halfway out the door. Blood was pouring out of a hole in his stomach, and his chest could have passed for a pin cushion.

"Oh, man," Zeus moaned. His stomach flip-flopped, and he thought he was going to be sick. He turned his head, and the nausea passed. When he looked up, McClane was kneeling next to the driver.

"What are you doing?" he asked.

"Interrogating him."

"What's he gonna say? 'I'm dead'?"

"Won't know till I ask," said McClane. "Check if there's aspirin in the glove compartment, will you?" McClane said, his head pounding.

Zeus glanced back at the poor bastard bleeding all over the dash. No way. "You check."

McClane ignored him. He emptied the terrorist's pockets. Another set of phony ID and union cards. And something else.

"Ten quarters," he said.

"What?"

"The guy in the dump truck had ten quarters," McClane reminded him. "Exactly."

Zeus shrugged. "Maybe they collect 'em."

"Yeah," McClane said, staring east towards Connecticut. "And maybe it's a bridge toll."

Chapter 9

"**W**alter!" yelled Kowalski. She waved to her boss, who stood huddled with Weiss and some of the other bomb-squad men.

Cobb and Weiss hurried down the hall to join her and Lambert, who'd been searching the school cafeteria. Lambert led them into the kitchen and over to the institution-sized refrigerators.

He pointed to the one on the end. "Janitor says this one was delivered this morning," he told them. "It's unplugged, right?"

Cobb nodded. "Yeah?"

"Look at the front," Lambert said.

The LED readout on the front of the refrigerator was functioning. Weiss and Cobb exchanged glances.

"We drill the hinges. Get everybody out," said Weiss.

Five minutes later, he was scanning the refrigerator door with an optic lens specially designed to scan through metal for explosives.

Cobb held his breath, waiting for Weiss's diagnosis.

"Not rigged. Pull it," he said.

Two bomb squad cops carefully removed the door and set it aside. Inside was a giant-sized version of the bomb that Weiss had brought into Cobb's office that morning: two huge translucent tanks of clear fluid, two smaller tanks of red fluid, all of them wired to a digital timer. The timer was ticking down the seconds: 20:23 . . . 20:22 . . . 20:21 . . . Next to the timer was a notebook-sized computer keyboard and a screen that read, DIS-ARMING CODE. The space where the code numbers should have appeared was blank.

Weiss sighed. He said, "You can call off your search."

Now driving the pickup, McClane was sure he'd guessed right. Simon's last stop before the gold left the United States had to be Bridgeport, Connecticut. The trucks had probably followed the same route he and Zeus had just driven: south from Danbury to Norwalk, where they would have picked up the Connecticut Turnpike. Otherwise known as I-95, the turnpike was a busy toll road that ate up lots of quarters and was the main

trucking route for commercial traffic between
New York and New Haven.

Bridgeport had the dual advantages of being a
working port that could handle a ship large
enough to suit Simon's needs and was far enough
away from New York that no connection would
be made between his cargo and the bombings.

McClane had to give him credit. The guy was
smart. But he was smarter. He tossed a quarter in
the exact change machine and sped onto one of
the twin bridges that spanned the harbor.

"There!" Zeus yelled. "Over there!"

A squad of dump trucks sat parked on one of
the wharfs. A ship was just pulling away from the
dock. A crane, which had no doubt been used to
load the gold aboard, jutted from the ship toward
the sky like a beckoning finger.

"They're on that ship! We're too late!" Zeus
cried.

They jumped out of the truck and ran to the
rail. The ship had already reached midway between the wharf and the bridge on which they
were parked.

"Shit!" McClane whirled around and
screamed at a passing motorist to get the police.

"Forget the goddamn phone! Find the cops!
Get them over here ASAP!" he told the man,
who looked uncertain about whether or not this
ranting lunatic should be taken seriously.

Zeus, meanwhile, stared over the side of the

rail, feeling increasingly helpless and frustrated as Simon's ship drew closer to the bridge.

Suddenly, the solution hit him like a jolt of electricity.

"I can jump!" he said. "I'm gonna jump to the ship!"

McClane shook his head. Zeus had kind of grown on him. After all they'd been through, he didn't want to watch the guy waste himself. "That's a hundred feet," he said, pointing at the ship's deck.

"Not to the crane, it isn't."

"You won't make the crane," said McClane, an idea beginning to take shape in his head.

"I ain't lettin' that bastard kill my nephews!" Zeus said, steeling himself to make the jump.

"Splashing yourself all over the deck ain't gonna help." He pulled Zeus away from the railing, moved around to the front of the pickup, and started uncoiling the cable wire from the winch on the truck's hood. "Stop talking crazy and see if you can find some gloves."

Gloves? Zeus was baffled. But so far, most of McClane's wacky schemes had been right on the money. A hundred feet was a long drop down. If McClane had a better way, he was all for taking it.

He went to rummage in the pickup and found a pair of utility gloves and a grease rag. When he came back around the front of the cab, McClane had unspooled about fifty feet of cable.

"How are you at fishing?" he asked, checking the hook at the end of the cable.

"Shitty," Zeus said.

"Me, too." McClane grinned. "All I ever caught was the clap." He peered over the side of the bridge. "Here goes."

He lowered the cable and waited until the ship began to pass beneath the bridge. He dropped the cable another foot and dangled it back and forth, maneuvering to get the hook to catch the top of the crane. He missed on the first try, because he'd swung the cable too far left. He corrected his error the second time and felt a tug as the hook wrapped itself around the crane.

Zeus watched the cable slipping out over the water. "Now what?" he asked.

"Wait for it to go horizontal and just climb on over." McClane winked at him. "Piece of cake. What'd you find for gloves?"

Zeus showed him what he'd come up with.

"What are you gonna do with that?" McClane poked scornfully at the grease rag.

"I'll make it."

"Yeah. With no hands."

He shoved the gloves back at Zeus. Then he slipped his holster harness off his shoulders, wrapped the leather around his hands, and positioned himself to climb over the rail and onto the cable.

Zeus grabbed his arm. "No, you don't," he protested. "I've been playing Tonto to you all day."

His idea, his turn to go first. He climbed onto the rail and let the cable slip through his gloved hand. Then he sat back and waited for the cable to level off.

McClane stared down at the blue-gray waters of the Long Island Sound. He'd been wanting to ask Zeus about something ever since he'd admitted to having been a crack addict. His timing might seem odd, but for reasons McClane didn't really understand, he had to know the answer.

"Tell me one thing," he said. "After you got your brother killed?"

Zeus glared at him, his eyes blazing with anger.

"Hey, a white cop pulled the trigger, but you got him killed. We both know that," McClane said.

Zeus hated hearing it, hated admitting it even more, but McClane was right. The plain and simple truth was that he was responsible for his brother's death.

"What I want to know is, how'd you put your life back together after a thing like that?" McClane asked.

The cable leveled off. Zeus readied himself to swing out onto it above the water.

"One fucking day at a time," he said. The hardest lesson he'd ever learned. The one that had kept him alive and sane.

With a prayer, he stepped off into space and began moving hand over hand toward the crane. The gloves helped some, but he could still feel the cable cutting into his palms, and the muscles in his arms and shoulders were already screaming in protest. As he torturously inched his way along the cable, grunting from the effort, he forced himself not to think about how far he would fall if he slipped.

When he reached what he figured to be the halfway mark, he made the mistake of glancing down at the ship. One of the terrorists had come up onto the portside stern deckhouse.

"Oh, shit," he hissed.

McClane, who was right behind him, followed his gaze. The terrorist hadn't spotted them yet. They were still safe. A second later, a sharp tug on the cable made him look back at the bridge. Forget safe. They were about to hit major trouble. The winch had run out of cable. The truck was being wrenched forward toward the water.

"Don't ask why. Just hurry," he yelled to Zeus.

The truck smashed headlong against the railing

of the bridge. The cable swayed as the railing began to buckle from the impact.

Their legs pumping, they scrambled to reach the crane before the cable gave way. They were over the stern, almost to their goal, when the terrorist happened to look up.

"Hey!" he shouted. He stared at them in amazement, then grabbed his machine gun.

Suspended above him, framed by the sky, they froze. Behind them, the railing snapped in half, collapsing under the weight of the truck.

The pickup arced downward, and the cable began to drop along with it. The truck hit the water with a resounding crack. The cable snapped and began to whip from side to side. It slapped the air and swung toward the stern. As the terrorist stood gawking, too stunned to react, the hook ripped into him. It snagged him like a fish on a lure and hurled him over the side.

McClane and Zeus went slamming into the crane. Zeus grabbed for it and held on tight. McClane's aim wasn't as good. He missed the crane and slid about four feet down the cable until he finally caught hold.

"Great fucking idea! Boy-o-boy! I sure am glad I didn't jump!" Zeus yelled, as he climbed down the side of the crane.

McClane followed him. His shoulder was a bloody mess of cable splinters. He was hurting so badly he didn't bother to tell Zeus to go fuck himself. This was a free country. He could have god-damned jumped if that's what he'd wanted to do.

He'd tell him so later. He had to save his energy now for more important things—like hiding the terrorist's body before any of his pals showed up.

"You take his feet!" he told Zeus. He grabbed the arms. They dragged the body across the deck and dumped it behind a pile of rigging.

McClane glanced at his watch. It was smashed to pieces. "What time you got?" he asked.

"Twelve minutes," Zeus said.

McClane picked up the terrorist's wrist and checked his watch. "He's got eleven. Let's hope he's fast."

Forget the talk. Zeus wanted to move. "Now what?" he demanded.

"Split up and search for Simon. This thing's got to have a ship-to-shore. We drag his ass to it and phone it in." As usual, McClane had the next step planned out and was ready to give the orders. "I'll try the cargo deck. You check the cabins."

He scooped up the terrorist's rifle and threw it to Zeus. "Take this."

Zeus grabbed for the rifle and held it away from him. "How does it work?" he asked nervously.

"You don't know how to shoot a gun?" McClane was incredulous.

"What?" Zeus glared at him. "You think

black people are born with a gun in their hand? Racist motherfucker!''

"Sue me," snapped McClane. But the comment stung. There was some truth to it, though he wasn't about to say so. He settled instead for a quick riflery lesson. "Look, you just yank this back, and pull the trigger."

"That's it?" said Zeus. He rested the stock on his shoulder and glanced along the barrel.

McClane nodded. "Try not to shoot yourself."

Zeus scowled at him as he headed off to find the cabins. But McClane couldn't let him leave without one last bit of instruction.

"Listen," he said. "If you find him, don't try to be a fucking hero. Come get me."

Cobb couldn't tear his eyes away from the bomb that Simon had planted in the refrigerator. His heart was pounding in rhythm with the timer, one beat for each passing second. "Can you stop it?" he asked Weiss.

"I shouldn't even touch it," Weiss said, nervously flexing his fingers. "Who knows what kind of booby traps it's got. What about the code?"

Damn McClane for not finding a way to get in touch. Cobb harbored a momentary image of him hanging around some bar, running up a tab. He shook his head. "No word."

Lambert had been pacing the cafeteria, chain-

smoking despite the ban on cigarettes in the
school building. "When do we evacuate?" he demanded.

"Simon said if he saw one kid leaving . . ."
Cobb reminded him.

Lambert had three kids who went to public
school in Queens. He kept seeing their faces
whenever he thought about the kids who were
gathered now in the auditorium, oblivious to the
drama being played out just next door to them.

"We're not gonna sit here with our thumbs up
our butts waiting for that thing to go up!" he protested.

Cobb weighed the choices and decided Lambert was right. McClane was a long shot to call in
with the code. They had to get the kids out of
the building in case Weiss couldn't dismantle the
bomb before the timer hit zero. One way or the
other, they were going to beat this goddamn
clock.

He decided that if anyone could get the kids to
listen up and behave, it was Kowalski. He quickly
consulted the principal, worked out a plan together with Kowalski and Lambert, then sent the
three of them over to the auditorium.

Lambert winced as they hurried up the aisle
toward the stage. A pretty young teacher was
standing at the front, leading the students in a ra-
cuous round of "Row, Row, Row Your Boat."
The noise level was off the scale.

The teacher managed a weak smile when she saw them coming. She held up her hand and signaled the children to stop singing. It took a few moments for them to get quiet. Then she said, "That was nice! And look who's here. Mrs. Martinez. Say, 'Hi, Principal Martinez.' "

"Hi, Principal Martinez," the kids echoed her, more or less in unison.

Mrs. Martinez clasped her hands in front of her and waited for them to fall silent again. Lambert was standing close enough to see that she was shaking with fear. But when she began to speak, her voice sounded calm and unconcerned.

"Mr. Lambert here is from the fire department," she said. "He's going to show us a new fire drill. So everybody up. We'll make a nice long line right over there."

The room got noisy again as the children stood up, scuffling their shoes and whispering among themselves about this exciting break in their routine. Following their teachers' directions, they began to form neat lines at the end of each row of seats.

Zeus's nephews, Dexter and Raymond, were seated next to each other at the back of the auditorium. "Fire drill my ass. That guy ain't from the fire department," Dexter said, pointing to Lambert.

Raymond gazed anxiously at his older brother. "You think it's about the stereo?"

"No," said Dexter, though he'd been wondering the very same thing himself.

The uncertainty in his tone was all the confirmation Raymond needed. He'd watched hundreds of cop shows. He knew just what would happen. They'd be arrested, hauled off to jail, fingerprinted, forced to sit for hours under bright lights, made to answer questions, and tell on each other. They'd maybe even have to go to court. Zeus would kill them.

They were dead meat unless they made a quick getaway now, before the cops grabbed them.

"Tony squealed! Come on!" he said.

Cobb hurried into the auditorium and found the students lined up in two groups at each of the exits. "I've got the janitors making a last sweep of the building," Mrs. Martinez advised him.

She'd sent them upstairs to check each of the classrooms, with instructions to lock the doors once they were sure that all the students were safely out. The janitors were well-meaning and conscientious, but they were worried about their own safety, as well as that of the children's. A quick glance inside each room—and then they closed the door and were gone.

Dexter, Raymond, and two other boys who had sneaked out of the auditorium with them had heard someone coming down the hall and hidden themselves behind the teacher's desk. They held their breaths as the footsteps stopped at their room. Then the door closed, and the footsteps moved on.

Raymond pumped his arm in the air. *Awright!* He pulled out a deck of cards and shuffled them. "Okay," he said. "Five card stud, three and nines wild."

Targo was by nature a deeply suspicious person. He trusted no one, with the exception of his bodyguard/assistant, Berndt. The two men had grown up together in Hungary and served side by side in the Hungarian army, where they'd learned how to make bombs and other high-octane instruments of destruction.

Targo was the smarter of the two, but Berndt had an uncanny talent for sniffing out trouble. Fiercely loyal to his boss, he was always alert for signs of treachery and double-dealing. He'd had his doubts about Simon since the beginning of the operation. But he'd kept them to himself and bided his time—until now.

He went searching for Targo and found him below deck, on his way to join Simon and Katya on the port side of the ship. "I found something you should see," he said.

Targo shook his head. "Not now. We're on the clock."

"It's important," said Berndt. He stubbornly planted his two-hundred pounds of solidly-muscled body in front of his boss to keep him from brushing past.

"What is so important?" Targo impatiently demanded.

Berndt opened his fist and offered him the lump of scrap iron he'd found in the hold. Targo frowned. Simon would have to wait. This did, indeed, warrant his personal investigation.

McClane had just reached the bottom rung of the ladder that led to the hold when one of the terrorists suddenly appeared through the darkness. The man stared at him in mute surprise.

"Which way's the casino?" said McClane.

The man grabbed for his gun. McClane was faster. Two quick shots, and Simon had lost another member of his team.

McClean left him lying at the foot of the ladder and hurried down the corridor, ducking further into the shadows as two more of Simon's men walked past.

The hold was dark, quiet, crowded with the containers that had earlier been loaded onto the ship. McClane kept his gun cocked as he crept between the containers, hoping to find Simon here among them. He figured he had eight, maybe nine minutes at the most, before the bomb would explode. He had to get the code so the bomb could be disarmed. If he was feeling really generous, he might let Simon live to rot in jail for the rest of his life, instead of blowing his brains out. Or maybe not.

He flattened himself against the wall, turned a corner, and discovered he had company. A big, beefy man—not Simon—suddenly blocked his way. He fired. The other man returned the fire. McClane dived behind a container and let loose three more shots that sent the man sprawling backwards onto the floor.

His gun still drawn, McClane leaned over to take a quick look at the terrorist. Satisfied that the guy wouldn't be causing anyone any more trouble, he turned around to continue the manhunt. He caught a fast glimpse of someone standing on the container above. He recognized the face from the FBI pictures. Targo!

Targo leaped into a karate kick. McClane dodged, but he wasn't fast enough. The boot caught him square in the face and sent him flying. His gun skidded away behind one of the containers. He grunted as Targo landed on top of him, wrestled his arms to the floor with one hand, and smashed his jaw with the other. The guy was a fucking animal. McClane had a strong hunch he was about to get the shit kicked out of him.

It was warm in the cafeteria, but Weiss wasn't sweating from the heat. He was used to working under pressure, but pressure had taken on a whole new meaning for him this afternoon. He'd begun trying to defuse the bomb by testing the circuits. But his tests weren't working.

"You are clever, aren't you?" he muttered.

He took a drink of ice water and dipped his sweaty hands in talcum powder to dry them. Then he picked up his wire cutters and began to snip. "Okay, honey. Let's dance," he said.

Next door, Lambert and Kowalski were each standing at one of the doors to the auditorium, facing the children who were lined up in single file.

"Okay, gang. In a minute, we're gonna have a sort of race," Lambert said. He smiled, reassuringly, he hoped, then turned to whisper to Cobb, "Walter, don't you think you're cutting this a little thin?"

Cobb glanced at his watch. Two and a half minutes to go. The kids were starting to get edgy. They could sense the tension in the air, and it was scaring them. He had to get them out now, while they were still calm enough to do as they were told. He couldn't wait any longer.

He nodded at Lambert and Kowalski. They threw open the doors. The courtyard lay beyond. A hundred yards to the street. Three hundred yards to safety.

"Okay!" Lambert yelled, trying to make a game of the evacuation. "When I say so, we're gonna run like crazy. We're gonna beat those other kids! Now, get ready! Let's go!"

The kids raced outside and across the courtyard. They were screaming and crying and shoving one another in their frenzy to put distance between themselves and whatever terrible thing was happening inside their school. Lambert and Kowalski rushed after them and grabbed some of the smaller children who had fallen to save them from getting trampled in the rush.

Uniformed cops who'd been stationed at the blue police barriers across the street ran to meet the children and hurry them out of range of the explosion. The last of the kids sprinted across the street.

Kowalski, Lambert, and Cobb looked up at the school, waiting to see whether Simon would make good on his threat. Nothing happened. No explosion. No flash of fire. No building toppling over from the force of the blast.

"Told you it was bull," Lambert said.

Cobb checked his watch again. "Time to get Charlie out," he said. He spoke into his headset. "Let's move, Charlie. Time's up."

"Gimme thirty seconds," Weiss replied.

He had already severed four of the wires. He had six more to cut—two minutes, four seconds to go on the timer.

"Takes a minute-fifteen if you're nine, Charlie. And last I looked, you weren't so light on your feet. Now move!" shouted Cobb.

"All right," he reluctantly agreed. But he sure
hated to give up now, when he was so close.

Cobb was about to give him one more warning
when Kowalski exclaimed, "Oh, my God!"

She pointed to the school, to a fourth-floor
window, where several boys stood with their
noses pressed against the glass.

"Christ! Tell 'em to get outta there!" Cobb
yelled.

"Dear God!" Mrs. Martinez cried. "I told the
janitors to lock the rooms!"

"Come on!" Kowalski screamed at Lambert.

One of the janitors waved at Lambert. "Hey!"
He tossed him a giant keyring as Lambert and
Kowalski raced toward the school.

Weiss was leaving the cafeteria when he heard
Cobb's part of the exchange coming over the intercom. "What's going on, Walter?" he asked.

He heard Cobb's heavy sigh, then, "We've got
kids still in the building."

That sealed it. "I'm staying," he told Cobb.

"No! Get outta there, Charlie!"

Weiss turned off his intercom and sat down
again in front of the bomb. He was going to finish
what he'd started, even if it was the last thing he
ever did.

Chapter 10

The portside corridors where Zeus had been searching for Simon were so quiet that he had started to wonder whether all the rats had jumped ship. He passed a row of empty cabins, climbed up one companionway and down another without seeing a soul. The place was deserted. No one was home.

He was about to give up and go find McClane when he suddenly heard the voice he come to know so well from his telephone calls. Simon was just around the corner, barking orders at someone. From the other end of the corridor, Zeus heard loud footsteps. He hoped they weren't coming in his direction.

His fingers tightened on the trigger of the rifle. He inhaled sharply and braced himself. He rounded the corner and saw the back of Simon's head.

"Don't fucking move!" he shouted.

Kowalski and Lambert raced up what felt like endless flights of stairs. They were sweating heavily and gasping for air by the time they reached the fourth floor. They could hear the kids yelling and banging on the door long before they got to their classroom.

Lambert fumbled with the key ring, madly trying to find the right key. "Fuck it!" he said finally and smashed open the door with his shoulder.

They grabbed the kids, and Kowalski started back toward the stairs.

"No time!" Lambert yelled. "Go for the roof! We'll jump to the next building!"

They hit the top of the stairs. A padlocked chain-link gate blocked off access to the roof. The kids, by now utterly terrified, began to cry. Lambert flung himself at the gate and scrambled up to the top, then hung there as Kowalski pushed the kids up so he could lift them over the other side.

Four flights below, Weiss looked up from his work and spoke softly into the intercom. "Where are they, Walter?"

"Still inside," said Cobb.

The timer was at one minute, fourteen seconds. Weiss took a deep breath, and dabbed more talcum powder on his hands. "No guts, no glory," he whispered.

Zeus aimed the rifle at the back of Simon's head. "Give me the code, goddamn it!" he growled.

Simon slowly swiveled around and stared at Zeus with barely concealed surprise. "I'm afraid that isn't possible," he said.

Zeus was about to ask him why the fuck not, but the question died on his tongue when he felt the cold hard steel of two gun barrels against his skull. The hammers clicked in unison.

"Put the gun down, tar baby," Simon said.

Zeus was too mad to be scared. He kept his finger on the trigger and said, "Fuck you, you East-Block-Aryan-Nazi motherfucker. You call in the code or I blow your sick white ass into the next world."

Simon stared hard at Zeus. His gaze shifted to the rifle. His eyes widened slightly, and then he smiled. Zeus was in way over his head. He didn't even know that the rifle's safety was still in the "safe" position. He was an amateur trying to be a hero. "Go ahead," he said contemptuously.

Zeus thought, *Fuck you*. The bastard deserved to die. He pulled the trigger. Nothing happened.

"You have to take the safety off," said Simon, grabbing the rifle out of his hands. He clicked it off, pointed the rifle at Zeus's leg, and fired. Zeus screamed in agony and crumpled to the ground at Simon's feet.

"See?" Simon said.

At twenty-eight seconds, Weiss was utterly lost. He was playing a game of Russian roulette, trying to figure out which of the four remaining wires to cut. At twenty-seven seconds, the bomb whirred into action. The red fluid began to spiral down into the tanks that held the clear liquid. Weiss closed his eyes, held his breath, and randomly chose to cut one of the wires. He opened his eyes. He was still alive. The school was still intact. The bomb was still ticking.

McClane broke free of Targo's choke hold. He scuttled across the floor on all fours to retrieve his gun. Before he could reach it, Targo was all over him again, hammering his back and neck and face with his fists. McClane bent his knee and blindly aimed for Targo's groin. Targo grunted and doubled over, giving McClane time to roll away and throw a hard right jab that caught Targo square on the chest. The blow would have flattened most other men. Targo barely seemed to feel its impact.

He recovered in an instant and belted McClane with an uppercut to his chin. McClane tasted the blood in his mouth and slammed a sharp hook into Targo's stomach. Targo reared up, grabbed

McClane by the throat, and clobbered him with a series of jabs to his face and head.

"I see you all day, little man," he yelled between punches. "And you don't go away."

"I'm the Energizer-fucking-Bunny," McClane gasped, trying to duck away from Targo's merciless right hand.

Targo slammed him against a bulkhead. McClane momentarily blacked out. When he came to, Targo belted him in the mouth. "What you going to do now?" he taunted him. He whacked him across the nose. "You going to arrest me?" Another crack on his cheek. "Huh, bunny?"

A whack to McClane's gut knocked the wind out of him. He went limp as a rag doll. Targo dropped him and went looking for McClane's gun.

McClane caught his breath. "No, I'm not gonna arrest you," he muttered.

He dragged himself to the far side of a huge container, where Targo couldn't see him. He stomped down on the cleat lock that kept the container anchored in place, snapping it free.

"I'm gonna fucking kill ya!" he said. He threw his weight behind the container. It went sliding along the rail on which it had been parked, rattling loudly as it gained momentum.

Targo whipped around as the container hurtled toward him. It was moving too fast for him to escape. It crashed against the wall with a resounding clang that reverberated through the hold, crushing Targo beneath its weight.

Battered and bloodied, McClane staggered over to Berndt and picked up his pistol. The magazine was full. Grateful for small favors, he limped through the door of the hold and up the stairs.

"No guts, no glory," Weiss told himself at twenty seconds on the timer. Three wires were still left attached to the side of the tank. He picked one and tried to snip it in half. It was too tough. He couldn't cut it. He bore down harder on the wire cutter. The plug flew out of the side of the tank. The liquid explosive spurted into the air, drenching him with the blood-red substance.

He tasted it on his lips and almost fell over in stunned surprise. "Pancake syrup?"

The timer hit zero.

McClane ducked through the door of the bridge and swept the room with his gun outstretched. No one was there. He went to the phone and punched zero for operator.

"Operator!" he said as soon as her voice came on the line. "This is McClane, NYPD. Get me the Coast Guard now! I don't care if all the lines are down!"

He nodded vigorously in answer to her question. "You're goddamn right it's an emergency!

I'm on a ship out in Long Island Sound with a bunch of terrorists and a couple of hundred billion in stolen gold.''

The woman was a dodo brain. ''Will I stay on the line? Where the hell do you think I'm going?''

While he waited for his connection, he scanned the room again. He glanced out the window toward the stern and almost dropped his gun in shock.

A bomb, almost identical to the one he'd found in the park, hovered above the open cargo hatch, suspended by a crane. Only difference was that this bomb was about ten times the size of the other one.

A piece of the puzzle clicked into place. ''Oh, shit,'' he mumbled.

He turned back to the phone. ''And honey?'' he said. ''While you're at it, tell 'em the bomb in the school's a fake. I'm staring at the real one.''

He looked up and discovered that he was surrounded by Simon's men, all of them armed. A woman he recognized as Katya marched the limping Zeus into the room, holding a gun to his head. Bringing up the procession was Simon. At last, they'd come face-to-face.

''Oh, my. What have you done?'' Simon said.

McClane could have ripped the guy's head off. But the forest of guns trained directly at him at his head discouraged him from making any sudden moves. He settled for telling him, "I've got a marine operator on the line, asshole. I just gave your game away."

"Thank you. I hope she's still there. It's been hell getting through on the phones," Simon said.

One of his henchman relieved McClane of his gun and muscled him over to stand next to Zeus, who had a tourniquet tied around his wounded leg.

Simon raised an eyebrow at McClane, as if to encourage him to pay attention. Then he said, "Operator? This is Simon Gruber. Yes, dear, one of the terrorists. Are you able to record this call? Then start doing so now, I have something rather important to say."

He unfolded a sheet of paper and began to read from it. "This is a communiqué from the Combatant Revolutionary Faction. We trust you found our little schoolyard prank amusing. What follows will not be. For too long, you in the West have successfully conspired to steal the wealth of the world, while consigning the balance of humanity to economic slavery and starvation. Today, at the request of my friends, we are going to level the playing field. In fifteen minutes, this ship and the entire contents of the Federal Reserve Bank, the gold that your lavish economies are built on, will be redistributed by explosive to the bottom of the ocean. You are cordially invited to come and watch."

He neatly refolded the paper and said to the operator, "Will you see that the authorities and the media receive this at once? Thank you, dear."

He hung up the phone and turned to his men. "Put the package in the hold," he instructed them. "Set the autopilot. Then get to the launch."

As the bomb disappeared from view into the hold, Simon and Katya led McClane and Zeus down to the cargo deck. By now, the bomb had been lashed to a bulkhead. Simon nodded at Katya.

Zeus gaped at her as she connected the wires and set the timer. "You're gonna just blow it all up?" he asked disbelievingly.

McClane shook his head. "I don't buy it."

"You don't have to," said Simon. "You'll be part of it. They'll be dredging the harbor for years. The markets will crumble in days. Try to imagine the price of oil west of Syria."

"This never had anything to do with killing kids," McClane said.

Simon feigned hurt feelings. "What sort of a monster do you think I am?"

"And this wasn't about your brother either?"

Simon laughed, a harsh, unpleasant snigger that made McClane's teeth ache with hatred. "Hans was a miscreant with little imagination. We weren't what you would call close."

"He was a miscreant and you're a psychopath,'' McClane shot back. "Sounds like a great fucking family. What was Mom like?''

His comment was a conversation-stopper. Simon stared at him in icy silence until Katya was finished rigging the bomb. Then he said, "Cuff them to the pipe.''

Katya was surprisingly strong—and rough. She slammed Zeus, then McClane, down onto the floor and shoved them against either side of the pipe. She forced their hands behind their backs, snapped handcuffs onto their wrists, and attached the cuffs to the pipe.

"Not so tight,'' said McClane.

Katya adjusted the cuffs so they fit even more tightly than before.

"Thanks, honey.'' He winced and turned to Simon. "I thought this wasn't about revenge.''

"You know, there's a difference between not liking one's brother . . . and not caring when some ignorant Irish flatfoot kills him,'' Simon said.

Zeus glared at him. "I never even met the guy,'' he complained.

Simon shrugged. "Just not your day. Have a short, happy life. Any last wishes?'' he asked McClane.

McClane remembered what the FBI guy had said about Simon getting migraines. "You got any aspirin? My head's killing me.''

Simon smiled. "Sure,'' he said expansively,

kneeling in front of McClane. He took a bottle out of his coat and stuffed it into McClane's shirt pocket. "Keep the bottle."

Simon was feeling extremely pleased with himself. All the elements were in place. He could not have hoped for a more perfect outcome. He allowed himself the luxury of thinking about a celebration as he and Katya approached the ladder that would take them down to the launch that was waiting below.

Katya's foot was already on the first rung when a hatch opened a few feet away from them, and Targo pushed his way out onto the deck.

"Simon!" he called.

Simon had not expected to see Targo again. It was an unhappy development, a flaw in the smooth surface of his otherwise perfect pleasure. The gun in Targo's hand was particularly worrisome.

"Where is the gold?" Targo demanded.

Simon said nothing.

"He's betrayed us," Targo told Katya. "The containers are filled with this." He threw a hunk of the scrap metal Berndt had discovered onto the deck.

Katya had known this moment would come, and she was prepared for it. She looked from the scrap metal to Simon. She pointed her pearl-handled Walther automatic at Simon and stared at him. His eyes told her everything. She pulled the trigger, aimed, and fired. But it was Targo, not Simon, who took the bullets, all three of them, squarely in the chest.

"Shall we go?" said Simon.

Ever the gentleman, he offered her his arm as he escorted her down to the launch.

The scene was so familiar that McClane was starting to get bored. Zeus, himself, and a ticking timer with a bomb set to blow. The timer had just passed 9:27.

"Woke up this morning and felt just fine. Now, I'm gonna die with you and a hundred forty-six billion in gold. What a shitty, fucked-up day," Zeus said bitterly.

McClane had a news flash for him. "It's worse than that. You're only dying with me. The gold ain't on the boat."

"How the hell do you know that?" Zeus demanded.

" 'Cause I know this guy," McClane informed him. "I know the family. What's better than blowing up a hundred forty-six billion dollars? Making everyone think you did."

Zeus couldn't believe he was having this conversation. He was nine minutes away from passing to the Great Beyond, and McClane was filling him in on the Gruber family. "Then where is it?"

he asked, more to keep his mind off the bomb than because he gave a damn.

"He probably switched it back at the dock."

"That supposed to make me feel better?"

"No," McClane said. "The other part you were wrong about is we ain't gonna die."

Wrong-o. Not unless McClane's middle name was Houdini. "You know some cop trick about getting out of handcuffs?"

"Yeah, use the key. Can you pick the lock?"

"You think every black man in the world—"

"Shut the fuck up." If there was one thing McClane didn't want to hear right now, it was Zeus's rap about him being a racist. "Can you do it or not?"

"Yes, if I had something to do it with," Zeus admitted.

McClane looked at his raw, bleeding shoulder. A steel splinter was stuck about an inch deep into the skin. "Hang on," he said. He craned his neck, raised his shoulder, and grabbed the splinter between his teeth. He yanked hard and grunted. It hurt like hell. He extracted a two-inch piece of steel.

He clenched it between his teeth, then spat it over his shoulder to Zeus. "Try this," he said.

It was slow going. Zeus's hands were slippery with sweat. He was literally stabbing in the dark, working behind his own back on a lock he couldn't see. His hopes of escape quickly fading, he said, "As cops go, you're not so bad."

"Stop thinking we're gonna die. Besides, I lied to you."

Zeus peered around the pole at McClane. " 'Bout what?"

McClane decided to come clean. "The bomb Weiss found in that park in Harlem? It was really in Chinatown."

Zeus stared at him in disgust. "That was low. Even for a white motherfucker like you."

"I know. I'm an asshole," McClane said cheerfully. "But you weren't gonna come."

The timer flipped to two minutes. "You married, McClane?" Zeus asked, trying to distract himself with talk.

"Yeah." McClane nodded.

"Kids?"

"Yeah."

"Hard to imagine anyone putting up with you long enough to have kids," Zeus said.

"She barely did. We're separated." McClane thought about what Holly would say if he didn't make it off the ship. Sure, she'd be sad. She might even shed a few tears. She still loved him. He would have bet his detective's shield on that. "All she's gotta do is mail in the form."

Zeus felt the splinter hit one of the cylinders. "You don't sound too happy about it," he said.

"I'm not," McClane admitted.

"So tell her."

He wished he could. But it wasn't that simple. "We don't talk."

"Why the hell not?" Zeus asked, his shoulder beginning to cramp up from the strain on his arms.

"We got into a fight one night on the phone. Wanted to call her the next day, but I was still pissed off. I thought, you know, she can call me. Then a week went by. Then another. Been over a year now."

The words came spilling out before he could stop them. He hadn't told anyone else how things had gotten to be so bad between Holly and himself. Zeus was about the last person in the world he would have figured to spill his guts to. Still, he was glad he'd done it—until he realized that Zeus was laughing his head off.

Zeus couldn't help it. "You mean, you're gonna throw away your marriage and kids, screw up your whole life, just because you were too pissed-off to pick up the phone? That is the dumbest fucking thing I ever heard. Jesus Christ! White people. . . ."

He heard a noise—*clink!*

"Got it!" he suddenly exclaimed.

McClane's right handcuff snapped open. McClane jumped up and snapped the cuff on his left wrist, getting it out of the way.

"Shit," said Zeus.

"What?"

"The thing broke. You got another one?"

"No," McClane said. He glanced at the timer. 1:28.

Zeus made up his mind. "Get out of here," he said.

"We gotta think of something."

"Go on!" Zeus urged him.

"I ain't leaving without you! And I don't intend to die. So start thinking."

The timer hit 1:09.

Zeus had guessed right from the start that McClane was crazy. But he was a good kind of crazy. Especially for a white man—and a cop. "Maybe there's some tools in the engine room," he said desperately.

McClane shook his head. "No time."

The timer hit 00:59. The red liquid began mixing with the clear.

"Shit!" said McClane. He did a quick check of the area. He found the solution—a pair of navigator's calipers—lying on a chart table.

He grabbed them and spun around to the bomb. He used the calipers to puncture a hole in the red tank, so that the liquid began to trickle out.

The timer hit 00:50.

Zeus's mouth was so dry, it felt as if it were stuffed with cotton. "What the hell are you doing?" he asked in a funny, high voice he didn't recognize.

"Getting you out of here," McClane said.

He punched a hole in the second tank. A few drops of the clear liquid seeped out. He very gently applied a drop of the red liquid to the caliper's right leg, then a drop of the clear liquid to the left leg.

"Oh, shit," said Zeus, remembering Charlie Weiss's graphic demonstration back at the police station of the combined power of the two liquids.

"Close your eyes," McClane said.

He turned away as he tapped the calipers onto the chain of Zeus's cuffs. *Boom!* The explosion was loud and smoky, but contained. The cuffs flew apart. And they were still alive. McClane hauled Zeus to his feet.

The timer hit 00:40.

"Let's get the fuck out of here," he said.

Both of them limping, they dragged each other through the door and up the stairs. Zeus stumbled and almost missed the top rung, but McClane grabbed him and pulled him up onto the deck. Together, they dashed as fast as they could for the stern. They climbed over the rail and dived off the side of the ship.

They were still in midair when the ship exploded. The shock wave hurtled them far out over the Long Island Sound. They hit the water with such violent force that they were both instantly knocked out. They sank, unconscious, many feet down below the surface. Debris from the blast rained down around them.

They floated amid the newly created saltwater junkyard. McClane was the first to stir. He came to, flailing his arms, fighting for air, dazed and confused. Looking up, he saw rays of sunlight, weakly penetrating the watery depths.

He paddled over to Zeus and shook him back into awareness. The underwater universe was so peaceful and soothing. Their own world seemed so very far away as they began to swim toward the light. Fighting the temptation to surrender to the water, they rose up and up and up.

They broke the surface, spewing water and seaweed. They could see nothing for miles around, except water and smoke and pieces of wreckage that were all that was left of Simon's ship.

Chapter 11

A soft snow was falling on the quaint, medieval town of Bistrita, Hungary. People strolled unhurriedly among its cobblestone streets, pausing to chat with friends or to run an errand in one of the pleasant little shops clustered around the main square.

But for the occasional car driving down the narrow, winding streets, Bistrita could have been taken for a remnant of a previous century. It had been spared the hustle and bustle of modern, cosmopolitan cities. Unspoiled and peaceful, it was a sanctuary for those who preferred a quieter existence, a retreat from the stresses and strains of the world outside its heavy stone walls.

At the center of the square was the baroque-style castle whose towers could be seen for many miles around the countryside. Across from the castle was an unpretentious tavern, a favorite local meeting place where regular patrons were welcome to sit undisturbed for hours, reading their newspapers or playing extended games of chess.

On this snowy afternoon in December, the tavern was almost empty, except for one table where a group of men lingered over their beers as they noisily finished a hand of baccarat. One other table was also occupied. A man sat there alone, his face hidden behind his newspaper.

"*Itt a Conyakja uram,*" said the waitress, addressing the man in Hungarian. Here was his cognac. He didn't need to specify which brand. He came to drink here often, and to while away an otherwise dull afternoon.

Simon Gruber lowered his newspaper and smiled at the waitress. "*Nagyon kedves, Koszonam,*" he said.

She blushed, appreciating the compliment. Not too many customers tipped so generously, or bothered to tell her she was very kind to bring him his order. She put a glass down on the table, along with a bottle of cognac—from the customer's own private stock—and went back to the bar.

The bell above the door jingled as another customer came through the door.

Simon stubbed out his cigarette and poured himself a drink. When he looked up, John McClane was standing in front of him.

McClane picked up the bottle and examined

the label. "Louis XIII. A hundred bucks a glass," he said.

Simon did a quick survey of the tavern. Was McClane alone? Only partly reassured that he hadn't found any unfamiliar faces staring back at him, he said, "May I pour you one?"

"I quit," said McClane, pulling out a chair to join him at the table.

Simon stared at him as if he were seeing a ghost. "You're looking remarkably . . . alive, John," he said.

McClane said nothing. He was alive, no thanks to Simon.

"Fit. Even healthy," Simon said, his tone more clipped than normal. "How is Cobb? And your friends on the police?"

McClane noticed that Simon was rubbing his temples. Maybe his excitement about their reunion was giving him a headache. "They canned me. Cobb's trying to save my pension," he said.

"I'm sorry to hear that."

McClane didn't believe him. He didn't sound sympathetic. "The FBI even suspected I was in on it. Made me take a lie detector."

Simon's lips creased in a thin smile. "Ah. That's funny."

"I'm not laughing," McClane told him.

"Life's little ironies should be enjoyed, John." He pressed the heel of his palm against his forehead. "And Zeus?"

"Fine. His nephews made the honor roll."

Simon scanned the bar again. "You had children, too, John, didn't you?"

"Yeah. I'm seeing 'em next week for Christmas."

"And the point of your visit here?"

McClane tried not to look at the cognac bottle. He'd been sober almost six months, but some days the urge to drink was almost unbearable. "Gotta hand it to you," he said. "You beat everybody. Me, the cops, the Feds, your terrorist friends. Even walked off with the girl. Or did you double cross her, too?"

"Let's say her conversation was limited," Simon said. This time his smile looked less forced.

"You almost got away with it."

"But I did get away with it, John. Oh, I suppose your Navy may dredge up the gold over the next decade, but—"

McClane shook his head. "They're not going to find anything."

A long pause followed. McClane guessed that Simon was wondering how much he knew. He pulled out a small statue of the Empire State Building, the kind that all the New York souvenir stores carried, and scuffed it against the edge of the table. When he turned it over, the bottom of the statue gleamed with gold.

"The gold wasn't on that ship. You drove it

where? North?'' He'd had plenty of time to think about this. He gave Simon his best guess. ''Canada?''

''Congratulations. Nova Scotia,'' Simon said tersely.

''Melted it into trinkets and shipped it out.''

Simon pulled out his cellular phone and punched in a series of numbers.

McClane grinned. Simon was still playing with telephones. ''Don't bother. Two are dead and the other two are cuffed in the warehouse down the street,'' he said.

The phone went back into the pocket. McClane was prepared for what almost came next.

''Uh-uh,'' he said, as Simon reached for the gun under his jacket. He raised his own gun from beneath the table. ''Toss it over there.''

The bartender, waitress, and customers all froze in their places as Simon's gun clattered across the floor. The bartender dropped the glass he'd been wiping. It shattered loudly against the bar.

''Tell them to get out,'' McClane said.

''*Vesszeteki el*,'' Simon said.

He wanted them to leave? They were happy to go. The bartender motioned to the customers, who were already hurrying for the door.

The tavern emptied out quickly. The snow had stopped, and sunlight filtered through the windows. Simon squinted uncomfortably and rubbed his temples again.

"How long have you been here?" he asked.

He didn't sound as if he were asking just to make friendly conversation.

"A week."

Simon winced. McClane asked, "Are you in pain? Do you have a headache?" He pulled out a bottle of aspirins and slid it across the table.

"It's a German pharmaceutical company. I traced the batch number. That particular bottle was from a shipment sent to the pharmacy around the corner." He grinned. He'd waited months for this moment. "I'm a cop, shithead. C'mon, enjoy life's little ironies."

Simon's face was contorted with pain. He couldn't seem to stop rubbing his temples. He kept swallowing hard, as if he were about to be sick to his stomach. "What are you going to do?" he said, nervously licking his lips.

"We." McClane corrected him.

"What are *we* going to do?"

"Play a game. Called Simon Says." He reached into his coat and pulled out a green metal tube, two feet long and two inches in diameter. He set the tube on the table. One end pointed at McClane, the other at Simon.

"You've seen these before. Little Chinese rocket-launcher. Afganis used to love them. Simon says put your hand on the trigger."

Simon put his hand on the tigger. "You've pulled the sights and the directional arrows off, John. How can I tell which end will fire?"

"You can't." He pointed the gun at Simon's head. "Pop quiz. Answer all the questions, I tell you. You got thirty seconds."

Simon stared at the mortar. His left eyebrow twitched, betraying his tension.

Zeus's nephews had taught McClane all their favorite riddles. He wished Zeus were here with him now to enjoy the moment.

"Simon says, if a plane crashes on the Texas-Oklahoma border, where would the survivors be buried?"

"It's against the law to bury the living," said Simon.

"Good. Turn the mortar."

Simon reversed the direction and stared at Mc-Clane, trying to find the answer in his eyes. McClane kept his gaze blank, showing nothing.

"Simon says, how far can a dog run into the woods?"

"Halfway," said Simon. "After that he's running out of the woods." It was chilly in the tavern, but sweat beaded his forehead. He started to turn the mortar around again, hesitated, then finished what he'd began.

"Simon says, a cowboy rides eighteen hours to town and eighteen back, all on Sunday. How?"

Simon was silent.

"How?" McClane demanded.

He'd stumped the star. Simon's hand was shaking as he fiddled with the mortar trigger.

"How, shithead?" yelled McClane.

The answer came to him. He breathed out a whoosh of relief. "Sunday's the name of the horse."

He turned the mortar around again. He studied McClane's face. It gave him no hints, not even the slightest clue. Simon couldn't tear his eyes away from McClane's. He was sure the answer to the riddle of the mortar was there, if only he looked hard enough.

McClane glanced nervously at the mortar.

Simon smiled. The policeman had betrayed himself, as Simon had known he would. He spun the mortar around and pulled the trigger.

Fake out.

The tube exploded in Simon's face with a blinding flash of gunpowder that blew him out of his seat and sent him crashing backward against the far wall. Bits of flesh and pulverized organs splattered across the bar. A severed hand landed on one of the tables. A pool of blood began to seep out from beneath his body.

McClane stood up wearily and removed his coat. Under it, he was wearing a heavy flak jacket, which he stripped off and threw on the table. He took one last look at what remained of Simon Gruber.

He had one more piece of advice for him: "Never drink Napoleon brandy without a flak jacket."

Alcatraz. The prison fortress off the coast of San Francisco. No man had gotten out alive before his time was up, until a 20-year-old petty thief named Willie Moore broke out.

Recaptured, then thrown into a pitch-black hellhole for three agonizing years, Willie is driven to near-madness—and finally to a brutal killing. Now, up on first-degree murder charges, he must wrestle with his nightmares and forge an alliance with Henry Davidson, the embattled lawyer who will risk losing his career and the woman he loves in a desperate bid to save Willie from the gas chamber.

Together, Willie and Henry will dare the most impossible act of all: get Willie off on a savage crime that the system drove him to commit— and put Alcatraz itself on trial.

MURDER
IN THE FIRST

DAN GORDON

NOW A MAJOR MOTION PICTURE STARRING CHRISTIAN SLATER, KEVIN BACON, AND GARY OLDMAN